ON ELEGANCE WHILE SLEEPING

Originally published in Spanish as *De la elegancia mientras se duerme*
by Editorial Excelsior, Paris, 1925
Introduction copyright © 1995 by Celina Manzoni
Translation copyright © 2010 by Idra Novey
Introduction translation copyright © 2010 by Rhett McNeil
First edition, 2010
Second printing, 2011

Library of Congress Cataloging-in-Publication Data

Lascano Tegui, Emilio, Vizconde de, 1887-1966.
[De la elegancia mientras se duerme. English]
On elegance while sleeping / Emilio Lascano Tegui ; Translated by Idra Novey ;
Introduction by Celina Manzoni.
p. cm.
Originally published in Spanish: De la elegancia mientras se duerme,
Paris : Editorial Excelsior,1925.
ISBN 978-1-56478-604-3 (pbk. : alk. paper)
I. Novey, Idra. II. Title.
PQ7797.L29D4 2010
863'.62--dc22
2010033987

Partially funded by the University of Illinois at Urbana-Champaign
and by a grant from the Illinois Arts Council, a state agency

This work was published within the framework of the
"Sur" Translation Support Program of the Ministry of Foreign Affairs,
International Trade and Worship of the Argentine Republic

www.dalkeyarchive.com

Cover: design and composition by Danielle Dutton, illustration by Nicholas Motte
Printed on permanent/durable acid-free paper and
bound in the United States of America

ON ELEGANCE WHILE SLEEPING
VISCOUNT LASCANO TEGUI

TRANSLATED BY IDRA NOVEY
INTRODUCTION BY CELINA MANZONI

DALKEY ARCHIVE PRESS
CHAMPAIGN AND LONDON

VISCOUNT LASCANO TEGUI AND *ON ELEGANCE WHILE SLEEPING*: THE FRINGES OF A POETICS

My interest in Lascano Tegui was piqued by a now-distant exchange of pleasantries (more social than literary) appearing in publications and magazines during the modernist period in that space we call Latin American. I like to recall, among many others, the image outlined by the editors of the Cuban weekly *Revista de Avance* in 1928, because it establishes what would practically become the model for describing Tegui thereafter:

> Viscount Lascano Tegui recently passed through Havana. He has the stocky build characteristic of the Argentine pampas, the smile of a *boulevardier*, and the skeptical eyes of a globetrotter. He devoured the ubiquitous stuffed crab at a local restaurant. He made the rounds on San Rafael and Galiano with his enormous Kodak camera. And he then regaled us with his magnificent hospitality, two hours full of refined humor and polished opinions on board the SS *Cap Polonio* [. . .] At the end of this visit from Lascano Tegui, one of the first Argentineans to give voice to "the new sensibility," we were left with abiding fond memories and a treasured copy of *On Elegance While Sleeping*. Safe travels for our good friend.[1]

---

1   *Revista de Avance*, 2:3, Feb. 15, 1928.

It's possible that this self-image was Lascano Tegui's first artistic creation, for not only did Tegui know how to make a name for himself wherever he went, he also managed to bestow a noble title upon himself, an audacity he shared with his neighbor on the other side of the Río de la Plata, in Uruguay: Isidore Ducasse, Comte de Lautréamont. The lofty, enigmatic Viscount seems to entirely overwhelm the humble Emilio we find on occasion in a few lines of the odd encyclopedia, full of erroneous bibliographic entries—as numerous as they are rare[2]—and almost always misquoted.

In addition to the list of verified titles Lascano Tegui published, starting in 1910—and which remained out of print even in Argentina until the nineties—there are references to other titles that are often quite difficult to verify. Furthermore, there is also a secret realm—a secret within the secret—made up of the articles published by Lascano Tegui in *Patoruzú*, a Buenos Aires magazine that was as widely read and popular as it was typically Porteño.

His reputation as major figure in the literary world of Buenos Aires is also corroborated in a speech that Norah Lange dedicated to the Viscount on September 10, 1936, at a reception marking the publication of his autobiographical novels *Album de Familia* (Family Album) and *El libro celeste* (The Heavenly

2 Not that the difficulty of obtaining them could ever overcome the desire to do so. Thus, when I presented a paper on Lascano Tegui at a conference called "The Atypicals," put together by the Institute for Hispanic American Literature, it was revealed that there were a number of secret admirers of Tegui who, until then, had been scattered and isolated among the ranks of professors, researchers, and students at the College of Philosophy and Arts at the University of Buenos Aires. I'm indebted to them for providing me with certain details of which I was previously unaware, and loaning me invaluable materials!

Book).[3] Even in Lange's objective, sardonic tone, one can sense—in addition to the affection she has for her good friend—that she feels slightly uneasy about the radical nature of Lascano Tegui's writing: she speaks of "psychosis" and "cerebral chaos," and one could almost say that she's a little envious of his mastery of "that delirium tremens for which we search in vain behind armoires, under the bed, and in the gaps of the crown molding."

While with other "atypical" writers the condition of being "unknown" usually carries with it an air of tragedy (as is the case with Pablo Palacio or Jacobo Fijman, for example, who died in mental hospitals, or with Edwin Elmore, the Peruvian, who was murdered by Santos Chocano), with Viscount Tegui one is surprised by his persistent youthful vigor—youth being the banner under which the early twentieth-century avant-gardists set out in pursuit of the new, of course, but which Tegui maintained, almost as an act of defiance, many years after the initial modernist fervor died down, in the pages of a publication that must have seemed far removed from the high-cultural headwinds of the time, and the happy few to whom his first books were dedicated.[4]

Between 1945 and 1951, Tegui published his weekly column in *Patoruzú*, on themes that must surely have surprised or at least perplexed his former colleagues, but which also must have

---

3   Lange, Norah. *Discursos*. Buenos Aires: Ediciones C.A.Y.D.E., 1942. pp. 43–45.

4   The dedications of those books reveal a circle of friendships and affinities that in 1926 was headed by Ricardo Güiraldes, alongside Girondo and Evar Méndez, and later, in 1936, would include Rogelio Yrurtia, Alfredo Palacios, Nerio Rojas, and Nicolás Coronado—under the spiritual patronage of Domingo French and Antonio Beruti—in a movement that seemed to shy away from the literary realm into a zone characterized by the confluence of art and politics.

entertained his new, expanded audience, due to his engaging treatment of the trivial: vacations, fashion, the weaknesses of a man in love, the automobile, banks, hats, streetcars, as well as proper etiquette, male flirtation, and grooming one's hands.

"On Manicures and the Sense of Touch"—issue 605, from May 1949—reasserts, albeit in very different genre and literary space, the sophisticated theme of the hand as a fetish object, or the fetishization of the hand, with which he begins *On Elegance While Sleeping*. In that article, the seasoned reader of Tegui will find a clear point of contact between his early novel and the later feuilletons.

On Elegance While Sleeping is presented as a personal diary, but it could also be read as a fictitious autobiography or a novel about origins, about initiation into the worlds of sex, literature, and crime. The choice of the diary as the form of the novel is justified by a certain structural aesthetic that dominates the text: that of fragmentation, instability, and changing perspectives. The convention of providing a date for each section, even though the dates are irregular, serves to mark limits, cutoffs, and pauses, and allows the narrator to jump from one subject to another without making the transition feel too abrupt.

Although this fragmentation is dictated by the conventions of the genre, it also justifies the changes in register: stories within stories, the evocation of memories, transcendental reflections, crisscrossing narrative voices, sequences that are interrupted as self-assuredly as they began; the transition from an elegiac to a sentimental tone, and from ironic to cynical; and the temporal fluctuation between a known past that is narrated—characteristic of autobiography—and the illusion of an immediate present in the diary itself.

Through this fragmentation, an apocryphal "I" is created, the apocryphal "I" of the author of the apocryphal diary, in an apocryphal time, characterized by a necessity of, or fondness for, disguise, change, and evolution. At one point a bout with typhoid fever leaves him bald; at another he is obliged to dye his red hair black to properly mourn his dead mother. His hatred of the daguerreotype—all the rage during the era the novel supposedly takes place—underscores his rejection of the fixed image. The narrator of the diary describes and constructs himself not as the static image of someone posing for a picture, characteristic of the nineteenth century, but as an image that prefigures the frantic movement of early cinema, even though literature is the model throughout; the narrator is reflected—and is brought to a logical conclusion—in the moving image of cinema.

The aesthetic of instability is also the aesthetic of arbitrariness and inversion: "The need for effects gave birth to stupendous causes," says the author of the diary. Instability, evolution, and transvestitism inform one of the central sequences of the text, about the seductiveness of homosexuality, of "inverted" sexuality. Balanced between fascination and fear, this sequence describes the trepidation of a man who feels that he is transforming into a woman under the amorous gaze of the other and constructs a story of a love unattained:

> At last I raised my eyes from their atonement and saw him looking at my hands, saw how, from his perspective, they must appear so soft and pink, how my lips were so red as to seem painted, how my clothes were of blue silk and my cuffs and collar made of lace.

The other man then leaves, and the narrator exaggeratedly reaffirms his masculine identity in a peculiar recounting of his sexual exploits, also characteristic of the personal diary. Literary treatment of this topic ranges in tone from the veiled references of a Sarmiento to the audacious declarations of a Lascano Tegui: "How many kilometers have I traveled in pursuit of a woman's breast!"

In other parts of the novel, the seductiveness of transvestitism and homosexuality is treated with contempt, in keeping with the reigning societal ethic, which today is quite difficult to comprehend. As such, the narrator establishes a parodic distance from homosexuality, resorting to the crudest naturalist tendencies. The stigma of the homosexual's condition is thus visible in his hands: "Have you ever seen anything quite so blunt yet unreliable as the thumbs of a sodomite? Next to the rest of their dapper, delicate hands, their thumbs stand out like bastards . . ."

For that reason the narrator proposes, "They should really only have four fingers on each hand."

The fragmentary nature of the text is intensified by the use of certain typographical features, chiefly the copious blank spaces and, in the original edition, the illustrations of Raúl Monsegur. Fragmentation, but also ambiguity; the ambiguity typical of a genre that pretends to be private, yet is made public. The illusion of authenticity that the canon bestows upon the personal diary (especially since the end of the nineteenth century) cannot conceal the paradoxical status engendered by the tension between the private and the public. Due to this tension, every personal diary that is published ends up negating itself as such; what is highlighted in this negation is the ambiguity of all literature and a disbelief in all literature that pretends to be realist or verisimilar.

Lascano Tegui also distances himself from the genre of the personal diary when he defines it at the end of the entry dated "September 4, 18—," one of the few occasions in which the text appears to deal with personal feelings:

> This page is inexplicable in the diary of my life. I've written it tenderly, as though I was once in love. It seems like sacrilege to include it as part of this intimate experiment, in which we're testing the consolatory effects of speaking badly about others to ourselves.

On the other hand, the novel's openness to the most seemingly trivial things—like the grooming of one's fingernails—illustrates two virtues that modern society tends to consider vices: the cult of idleness and the cult of the minimal. The very idea of a personal diary suggests that the text is composed of "idle" musings, or at least that it's the kind of book that is only possible when one has plenty of free time, plenty of time that isn't spent doing actual paid work; and when this impression is further confirmed by the fact that the book begins with an almost hyperrealist episode about a minimal detail like fingernails and fingernail clippings, the substitution of the ridiculous for the serious and the important seems assured.

At any rate, an unreliable autobiography that takes the form of a personal diary raises many questions. One has to do with what can be called the biographical and autobiographical impulse in Lascano Tegui. Indeed, one could read his *El libro celeste* (1936) as a biography of an entire country, with a focus on the Viscount's own particular autobiography, or read *El Muchacho de San Telmo* (*The Kid from San Telmo*, 1944) as an oscillation between this autobiography and the biography of a city, or at least one of its neighborhoods.

The violence of Lascano Tegui's gesture—the parodic appropriation of the genre of personal diary—might cause some initial perplexity and discouragement in a reader, perhaps exacerbated by the novel's focus on the trivial as the starting point for its "story." Furthermore, the novel is doubly removed from anything resembling a real diary, since the immediacy of what we expect from diaries—the sensation of living in the moment—is replaced by the defining trait of the genre of autobiography: recounting a life that has already been lived. "This journal I write, almost without wanting to, as dusk falls, doesn't always paint a true picture of what's happened to me. Rather, these are evocations of events, the memory of which passes its pen across my brow."

Within this space, this vacillation between genres, Tegui presents a personal history that is structured in such a way as to culminate with a crime (in this, the influence of de Quincey's "On Murder Considered as One of the Fine Arts" weighs heavily). The entire text moves in this direction. If all writing is displacement, transference, travel, movement, Lascano Tegui—great traveler that he is—constructs an itinerary that departs from what we'll call "the customs of the drowned" (taking a cue from Alfred Jarry) and travels toward the consummation of a gratuitous murder. The voyage begins earlier, however, with the manicure that readies those criminal hands and kicks off the trip:

> My hands no longer looked like they belonged to me. I put them on my table, in front of my mirror, and changed their positions in the light. With the same sense of self-

consciousness one feels when posing for a photographer, I picked up a pen and began to write.

That's how I started this book.

At the Moulin Rouge that night I heard a woman standing nearby say in Spanish: "He cares for his hands like a man preparing for a murder."

The depiction of the hand as fetish object runs through the entire book, from the hand that does the writing to the idea of writing as the consummation of a crime. Along the route that leads from the pencil to the dagger, the "theme of the hand" takes us down numerous detours—there is the fear of amputation in severed hands and severed genitals; hands that caress genitals, sometimes kindling fear and other times pleasure; the hands of the dead; hands with curative powers wearing black fingerless gloves or the clumsy hands that perform abortions; the hands of the drowned, upraised as if signaling for help; the hand of the onanist and the hand of the "sodomite." Tegui's image of death: "I've watched my family fall the way a leper watches his cold, swollen hands drop off in pieces."

The Viscount surprises us with the ephemeral, fragmentary quality conferred upon his text by the outrageousness of writing about serious subjects in a light, sardonic tone. The elegant tightrope act of narrating gratuitous crime, rape, abortion, homosexuality, the world of the brothel (an orientalized one, at that), the human body corrupted by illnesses: typhoid fever, tuberculosis, syphilis, insanity, leprosy; filth, misery, the secret and the shameful: everything that is not to be spoken of. This novel surprises us by the levity of its tone, as well as by something that

I would provisionally define as the intersection between a certain naturalist aesthetic and a pataphysical air.

And then it is also true that our Viscount crossed paths with the more working-class Roberto Arlt, who at this same time was publishing two prose pieces in *Proa*—the literary magazine run by Jorge Luis Borges, Brandan Caraffa, Ricardo Güiraldes, and Pablo Rojas Paz—which would eventually become two chapters of the famous *Mad Toy* (1926).

There are mysterious points of contact between Arlt and Lascano Tegui, as well as differences that may prove relevant: whereas Arlt works with some seriousness, the Viscount adopts the guise of frivolity. They can be read as two contemporary yet divergent aesthetics, products of the same period pointing to two different literary spaces. On the one hand, sex and money: a poetics of labor. On the other hand, sex and idleness: a poetics of *laissez faire*. A willful misreading. One wonders if the secret to Lascano Tegui's writings might also lie in a willful misreading.

CELINA MANZONI

UNIVERSITY OF BUENOS AIRES

Translated by Rhett McNeil

I write out of pure voluptuousness, I confess. I write for myself and for friends. I don't have a large audience or fame and don't receive awards. I know all the literary strategies intimately and despise them. The naïveté of my contemporaries pains me, but I respect it. I'm also conceited enough to believe I never repeat myself or steal from other writers, to believe I'll always remain a virgin, and this narcissism doesn't come cheap. I have to suffer the indifference of those around me. But, as I said, I write out of pure voluptuousness. And so, like a courtesan, I'll take my sweet time, and begin by kicking off my shoe.

VISCOUNT LASCANO TEGUI

ON ELEGANCE WHILE SLEEPING

The first time I entrusted my hands to a manicurist was the evening I was headed to the Moulin Rouge. The woman trimmed back my cuticles and polished my nails with an emery board. Then she filed them to points and finished up with some polish. My hands no longer looked like they belonged to me. I put them on my table, in front of my mirror, and changed their positions in the light. With the same sense of self-consciousness one feels when posing for a photographer, I picked up a pen and began to write.

That's how I started this book.

At the Moulin Rouge that night I heard a woman standing nearby say in Spanish: "He cares for his hands like a man preparing for a murder."

I was born in Bougival. The Seine flows through our village. Fleeing from Paris. Its dark green waters drag in the
grime from that happy city. As the river crossed our town,
it jammed the millwheel with the bodies of drowning victims,
bashful beneath its surface. One last shove and their journeys
were at an end. But they couldn't pass through the sluice gates
under the mill, and so it happened, on occasion, that one of
their arms would go through without them—and be seen
reaching into the air, as if for help. As a child, I fished out a
number of these bodies. There was a mailman in town who
was famous locally for always being the one to deliver news of
a death; I soon developed a similar sort of notoriety, becoming known for having discovered the most cadavers. It gave
me a certain distinction among my comrades, and I prided

myself on this honor. I threatened the other children that I would soon find them as well—the day they drowned. They'd tilt their heads, imagining themselves tangled in the sluices beneath the mill. My authority was beyond question: I had, in making my grim prediction, planted an inkling of tragedy into everyday life; which is precisely where logic will say it belongs, once the works of Aeschylus have been thoroughly assimilated into human consciousness, and seem as ordinary and simple as a schoolboy's composition . . .

Given the pressure and demands of my strange vocation, I became more preoccupied than anyone with the reputation it brought me. When I fished, which was often, I'd cast my line near the mill. I never looked at my cork, the rough current biting into it. All I was waiting for was the sight of a hand sticking up between the sluice gates. If I took a stroll, it was by the mill, and when they cleaned the machinery, I was the first to go down to the drainage cellars to examine the sludge that collected there, picking through the endless species of objects the river had dragged in—tired of its burden, relieving itself of its cargo under bridges and in the swamps along its banks.

The mill was old. It dated back to the time of Louis XIV, "the high priest of the classic wig," as I believe Thackeray called him—the man who, when he came to Marly, couldn't stop leaning out of his sedan to smile at the miller's wife.

In those days, millers' wives were known to be the most beautiful and flirtatious women in town.

During the Revolution, the Lord of Bougival asked the miller for asylum. Back then, millers held the keys to the nobility's

5

storehouses, and thus too served as their greediest customs men. The millers were also thieves, as a rule—stealing from the lords whose goods were in their keeping. But this particular miller surpassed himself: once he'd seen the tyrannical face of the royal house of France consumed in a bonfire on a certain gray autumn afternoon—I direct you to Rivarol's majestic description of that day—leaving the château in the hands of the *sans-culottes*, he agreed to save his master and took him down to the mill cellar on the pretext of hiding him there. The miller left the task of opening the sluice gates to his wife. The Lord of Bougival didn't scream. The waters took him, strangling him against the iron gratings; his body was torn apart, piece by piece, over the course of several months. A period during which nobody was particularly interested in watching the river as it flowed past the mill. The Lord of Bougival's arm reached out in vain.

When my mother died, my father, who was busy dyeing his sideburns, looked me over from head to toe and, finding my hair wasn't sufficiently serious for the occasion, dyed it black. Then he dyed my eyebrows as well, which had been carrot-red till then. This combined with my mourner's clothes made me look entirely different—like some newly discovered, hysterically melodramatic cousin. I saw just the type in a Daumier sketch soon after. I was horrified. That very day, I began to undermine my appearance—changing it gradually, quietly. Books played a large part in these transformations. I'd begin to adopt the wardrobe of one of the characters in whatever novel I was reading . . . and then switch models. Though I wouldn't have been able to articulate this at the time, I wanted to strip myself of every sign that would enable people to identify me with certainty. How I hated the static images of the daguerreotypes that were then so popular in my town—the poor villagers loved the sense of permanence they saw in those pictures, salivating over the shiny copper daguerreotype plates like middle-aged bourgeois types do over gold pocket watches . . .

And yet, the continual evolution of my appearance in those days did have lasting consequences . . . such instability jolted my inner self, leaving it forever unstable, easily jangled, always rattling around inside me like the clapper inside a bell.

I've returned from seeing the two white goats. One of them looked at me. She had the eyes of a lovely *señorita*. The afternoon had gotten quiet, and I felt a billy goat inside me who understood her. Goats are the animals I feel closest to, so I could hardly avoid returning her stare and walking over to get to know the more beautiful of the pair a little better—her pink udder like a woman's breast.

Today I threw a handful of hollyhock leaves at my *señorita*. She looked at me deeply before she gathered up the leaves, as if trying to understand the motives behind such obsequiousness. How similar she is to our provincial girls, pinning their hopes on every man who passes through town! Even the most despicable men—the girls stare at them all equally, and with such earnest longing, the same way prostitutes stare in the city!

That sort of look makes me fall all the more deeply in love. I've never felt such a desire to kick down a door or jump over a wall.

I followed the girl leading the two goats to graze by the river. My goat is named Isolina. She kept turning around; she knew I was watching. She moved her belly and udder most voluptuously. She was so busy watching me she didn't have a chance to graze. She went over to the daisies, broke off some stems, then abandoned them. When I left, she remained there, sad, at the steep edge of a gully. Her sister, who must care deeply for her, came by and licked her belly and udder.

Since I no longer had a mother, I didn't have anyone to help me maintain some level of communication with my elders. As a child, there were very few people I could ask for advice, who would offer me their wisdom and experience. Older people often lose the habit of interacting with children. They don't know how to talk to them and know even less how to understand them. Being impressionable, children tolerate them, but later come to hate them. Such children get used to living among other children alone. Until, and it happens from time to time, an ambassador from the adult world passes through. It's nearly always some old bachelor with the heart of a mother. A man who leaves his mark in all our alleyways, gets drunk in all our bars, and, in the end—as one takes home a souvenir to remember Venice—absconds with the mayor's daughter when he leaves. Thanks to a man like this, a painter, a man from the outside world, I first experienced fear and trembling. Above all, he taught how to understand these sensations. But he didn't come by night, dressed up like some bogeyman. No. I found myself in front of his house one morning. I had my hands in my pockets, my head was raised; I was whistling:

Ninon a des boucles d'or

The man saw me. Stopped. He stared at me with such interest that I could only feel flattered. Here, at last, was a man with whom one could have a conversation!

"What's your problem?" he asked. "Lose your hands?"

"Lose my hands?" I repeated to myself, feeling them in my pockets, experiencing a first little tremor of anxiety. The painter went on in that curious tone of his, sympathetic and deferential:

"Maybe they cut yours off?"

My trembling intensified. I started to shake and sweat, to feel cold, imagining myself without hands, both of them cut off by the butcher and hanging from two hooks like giblets. Unsure of myself, of my memory, I took my hands out of my pockets and looked at them.

They were still there at the ends of my arms, to be sure, but I was too startled to trust what I saw and had to look at them a long time.

The painter moved on. He made me realize, at four years old, the drama, the pure voluptuousness of living—the drunken ecstasy of our brief lives.

My neighbor the painter, Truchet was his name, didn't merely introduce me to terror. His words, his questions—like his gifts—were all quite disquieting for a child. He never gave me a handful of coins for caramels, as men generally give to children. No, Truchet gave me broken watches, which I found far more interesting in their silence than if they'd actually functioned. I'd poke around in them for several days, and when I saw the painter next I'd tell him over and over: "Sir? You know the watch you gave me, sir? I opened it and now it's ticking."

Making a watch tick again was, for me, as empowering as being named Grand Inquisitor. I made what little good was left in the machinery work, and then filled the watchcase with oil. In the depths, below the oil, the gears gleamed, more golden now—the balance wheel a ring of fairies, its ruby jewel bearings the eyes of mermaids, mass produced and sold at retail.

Another gift from Truchet that was impossible to forget was several flags on little flagpoles. I learned geography from them. Truchet gave me a yellow one with a black eagle in the middle and told me it was the Japanese flag, since it was yellow . . .

Later he gave me a red one and told me it was a flag flown by Kaffirs who ate only raw meat. The cross of Saint George was sewn on it in one corner, blue over white. When I wanted to know the significance of this, he responded: "Don't worry about a little thing like that. Probably they just used an old bit of cloth to patch the thing in Manchester."

My sense of geography was quite fitting, for a Frenchman. Mr. Truchet was entirely to blame.

I imagined I was entering the Middle Ages whenever I entered a pharmacy: the pharmacist like the sages of those bygone days, his jars covered in Latin like the pages of a schoolbook. The Middle Ages were an orphan's childhood, after the world lost its Greek father and had to strike out on its own. The Middle Ages were our first firm step into Humanity. The pharmacist who has replaced the village healer has all the uncertainty of a transitional state. He's the sage of the Middle Ages advancing toward the role of the doctor. The Middle Ages meant the loss of Mercury's staff and with it, the wings of the ancient world. Where are those wings now? Where can you find them? In pharmacies.

The smell of pharmacies . . . what is it if not the smell of science in the Middle Ages? If not the smell of unguents and lard? And, here and there, the stench of sulfur?

Faust is there behind the rows of glass bottles. Is he compacting powders into tablets, or is he preparing Mesué's polychrest, which the soldiers under Francis I used to cure Naples virus?

When I ask the pharmacist in my village—who sells leeches, as in the Middle Ages—for a little cyanide, his eyes widen with surprise: a saint forced to contemplate heresy. The substance I've requested is dangerous indeed, an alchemical disaster—but really, I only use it to massage my scalp . . .

SEPTEMBER 26, 18—

This journal I write, almost without wanting to, as dusk
falls, doesn't always paint a true picture of what's happened to me. Rather, these are evocations of events, the
memory of which passes its pen across my brow.

At twelve, I came down with typhus. I think it happened
while fishing for corks in the Seine. I collected these and sold
them to the junk man when the weekend came. Jug corks were
of particular value. Here are the statistics: for every hundred
corks, six were from jugs, forty from champagne or wine bottles, the rest from medicine jars. I rescued these corks—having
traversed the sewers of Paris and bobbed forty-six kilometers
along the Seine—from floating into the ocean.

One of those corks must have given me typhus. My successor,
another village boy, got sick as well. The junk man always boiled
our corks before he resold them.

After a number of fantastic voyages through the feverish deliriums caused by an impossible temperature of nearly 44° Celsius—never before seen in a human being, drawing the curiosity of doctors and scholars from universities as far as Paris, Dijon, and Lille—I lost three kilos a day, and then all my hair. All the people I saw during my out-of-body experiences were also bald, for some reason. My hair grew even redder than before, and one of the doctors who thought me an ideal subject took it upon himself to demonstrate that, as I resided in Bougival, and Bougival was next to Le Croisic, a town where they grew prodigious amounts of carrots, the color of my hair had responded, in this new phase of growth, to the colorings inherent in my environment. In a word, the doctor wanted to prove that my reddish hair was a product of local horticulture.

It was this same doctor who acquainted me with the pleasures of scalp massage. I mean concoctions of ammonia, quinine, sulfuric lime, and above all, potassium anhydrite, which left me with green hair for several hours. Doctor Rochefort tried all sorts of chemical solutions on my head, but the results always ended up contradicting his theory. I don't know what he thought would happen.

Those concoctions made up a good part of the magic of my childhood—those strange formulas spilling over my scalp and tingling through my body. I don't believe in opium or morphine, and even ether leaves me fairly cold. Those applications of cyanide, however, are what gave me that latent tickle at the base of my neck; sometimes I'd scratch myself so often I'd break out in blisters. Vaseline with camphor did no good. Ethyl chloride, however, thanks to its average temperature of 40°C below zero, gave me a little relief, at least.

Ammonia massages were the only ones I could get at a moment's notice, given how easy it was to find a place that offered them. As a child, instead of going to the circus on Sundays, I would go to the barbershop. If my father gave me a franc, it was enough for three treatments, but because the alkali always left a dark greasy trace on the towels, I'd scrub my head with the day's newspaper before I left one barbershop for another. The fresh ink from the news would stain my hair so not even the towel betrayed me—and the barber wouldn't suspect anything about my hygiene either.

Only once did I give myself a sulfate of quinine treatment. I went to the hospital dispensary with a neighbor woman who was sleeping with the pharmacist, and got my hands on a jar with some quinine salts left in it. For ten days, my head was entirely numb. I'd go to bed without knowing whether my forehead was against the pillow or exposed to the air. My scalp was drunk.

The Middle Ages. Still? Yes, everything in that era had an obscure, sinister justification to it. All observation was still interwoven with faith, and faith is nothing more than atavistic fear, the instinctive cowardliness of man. If this fear could conceive of God, it could find a reason for anything—and everything had an explanation in the Middle Ages. The need for effects gave birth to stupendous causes. Children today understand this instinctively; they can only admire those obsolete causes, seeing such beauty in their inscrutability. People have lost the rhythm of the supernatural. Montaigne said:

> Myself passing by Vitry-le-François, saw a man the Bishop of Soissons had, in confirmation, called Germain, whom all the inhabitants of the place had known

to be a girl till two-and-twenty years of age, called Mary. He was, at the time of my being there, very full of beard, old, and not married. He told us, that by straining himself in a leap his male organs came out; and the girls of that place have, to this day, a song, wherein they advise one another not to take too great strides, for fear of being turned into men, as Mary Germain was.

Upon hearing Madame Roland had been executed, her husband, then in hiding on a farm, took off across the fields to commit suicide. A few peasants heard the shot. Another Girondist dead.

They buried him along the roadside, so close to the topsoil that children broke off little tree branches and played at who would have the courage to poke the cadaver first.

For a time, the corpse made the ground above it somewhat pliable. Until one sunny day it caved in. Over the next few months, this hole collected water, which the shepherds' mastiffs came to lap up with pleasure.

From birth I've felt the desire to improve human nature, which makes us all so fragile and imperfect. I've sanctified my life to this sole endeavor. Logic hasn't aided my efforts. Logic must resist the same imperfections: it's also human. Logic decrees, for instance, that you pour water over a fire to extinguish it. Myself, I've attempted to put out fires by carrying a flask inside a satchel.

I haven't been successful.

What I have retained despite this failure is the consolation of having rehearsed a personal procedure, and one that isn't necessarily beholden to the logic of men who, while they may know how to put out a fire, don't know, conversely, how to be happy. I've always wanted to be happy. It was necessary to follow another path.

I didn't discuss the problem with anyone. The notion of happiness no longer seems to be in fashion. But I've asked myself: Do I have a soul? And answered: Yes. Then, what is it? An imperceptible silhouette, following me about—external, seamless, vaporous, etcetera? No, these are simply more assumptions based on our flawed human logic. Spirit cannot be separated from matter; spirit *is* matter, or else it cannot have a life, color, shape, or anything else. The logic of man is the logic of the children of Macedonia, who are born philosophers—same as the children of Manaus (Brazil).

~

My mother cut and stitched our clothing but never sewed on our initials or put any more care into our shirts than she would into the hem of a kitchen rag. Despite her being rather uncouth, I grew strong and healthy, same as my poor brother—who later proved useful as a medical experiment.

Our dutiful mother had an artist's temperament, I think, which was why she kept our clothing simple. I would like to compose these notes in the same straightforward way—with her same sincerity and plainness.

We had a large carriage depot in Bougival. Come evening, these heretofore idle carriages would depart for Paris. They were our town's only night owls. In a café, "Au Rendez-vous des chochers," the drivers would get together for wine. Among those wide, paunchy men with their flushed faces, I met one who was exceptionally wide, paunchy, and flushed: his face was a beet with two little holes that opened to allow his eyes to peer out. On top of that, these eyes hid under a single eyebrow, like the forehead-strap on a muzzle.

The man was a rag torn off some holy cassock. A defrocked priest. He took me along with him until the road to Mont Valérien sometimes, recounting the secrets of his adventurous life as a coachman, enjoying himself immensely, as if he thought of himself as one of the Eugéne Sue characters that appeared weekly in the newspaper serials. On one of these trips, he told me this story, which clarified certain mysteries of his life:

"I was excommunicated by the Bishop of Orléans. A complete bastard. And then, one night at the Gare d'Austerlitz, this same bishop hails me and climbs into my coach and makes me drive him to a house on the outskirts of Paris. When we arrive, he steps out and asks me to wait."

On the way to the house, the coachman longs to strangle his passenger. He moves along the streets waiting to feel the courage he doesn't have, and as night falls, vengeance lights up his heart like the red lantern in his rickety carriage. I refer of course to that same heart that had previously been offered up to God upon the modest altar of his village parish. To the Villager God, carved in wood and painted with lime. But fat had made the excommunicated friar into a sweet man in the meantime. Inclemency had ennobled him, like the golden sprig of wheat hidden under a poverty of rotting hay. The coachman is incapable of putting an end to that tyrannical bishop, his enemy sitting comfortably just behind him on the cushions of his cab. When they finally arrive at their destination, the old bishop, in his full priestly attire, descends ceremoniously, perfumed with incense and rustling his silken vestments. He proceeds slowly up the steps of the house that awaits him.

Our driver searches for a nearby shop and buys some bread and cheese for his dinner. His fare continues to keep him waiting, though it's already ten at night. All of a sudden, a frantic woman runs down the house's front stairs shouting for help. The coachman leaps down.

"Dead! . . . Dead!" the crazed woman cries and disappears into the shadows at the end of the street. And that's it.

No sound, no door creaking on its hinges, no other voices. The house is numb with death. Our driver leaves the snack he's just started, along with his life after excommunication, spent over the coachbox, and begins to climb the stairs.

On the second-floor landing, a door opens. He enters and continues down a hallway covered with the scattered clothes of a person who was in a hurry to disrobe and at last reaches a lit room. Here there's a bed and a stiff on the bed, his shirt half-opened, his stockings still on: the Monsignor in his final sleep. The room is full of fabulous colors—red, white, violet in all its splendor, the green of the bishop's stockings, and just above the stockings an array of mixed-tone sores that run like buckles along the holy man's disreputable calves. On his red and gray chest—gray from all the pale hair covering it—a string of silver medallions and gold gypsy coins. The terrible light of a single candle puts a halo of light over the bishop's amethyst episcopal ring and a warm glow over the skin of his sex. Vomit, uneven in color, sullies the corpse's head. His cassock would've fallen to the floor but has been held in place with a silvery rope. His skullcap sits on the night table with his pocket watch inside. Somehow, thanks perhaps to a trick of the light, everything around the corpse looks just as dead as he.

"Then, you see, from behind the drapes, came a sound like a cat that's fallen asleep on a newspaper, changing its position. The bed creaked. The organdy curtains trembled. A slim woman emerged from between their bright damask pleats. My presence scared her out of her wits and she fled the room, clutching her breast, running right past me and down the corridor, letting out a startled scream: *Mama!*

"Her voice carried up through the house. I heard someone else running—the steps seemed to be coming from the ceiling. An older woman with a decisive air appeared then in the doorway. In one look, she took in the scene. No hesitation. She knew perfectly well what had to be done in difficult situations such as these, as though she'd already had a troupe of daughters inducted into Paris Opéra Ballet (excellent training, then as now, since—as I'm sure you know!—the Opéra is absolutely the last word in upper-class bordellos) . . .

"'Help me,' she said.

"We tossed the body onto the carpet next to the bed and then dragged the bishop into the living room. We began to dress him there, putting on his skullcap just so and placing his pocket watch at his side. With great effort, we managed to get the corpse seated in the armchair next to the piano.

"The cadaver still hadn't stiffened. He yielded gallantly to our efforts, as though apologizing for the disaster, while we did with him whatever seemed best. The mother, whose features to my now fairly sympathetic eyes were becoming more and more aristocratic by the minute, picked up a musical score and placed it in the bishop's hands. When we propped him back against the headrest, the departed released one final mouthful of minced chard he'd been saving in his stomach, and it spattered all over the music.

"The Curia, to which the young maid had run when she bolted from the house, sent three novices in black. Improvising, they entered skinny and solemn into the Louis Philippe-styled salon. One of them stayed to guard the door. Another headed to the right to get a good look at the scene of the crime. The third went straight to the cadaver.

" 'Could you please go over the sequence of events?' this inquisitive one asked, like a detective.

" 'It's all quite clear,' the lady of the house replied—her performance almost stage-worthy. 'My daughter was at the piano,' she said. 'Monsignor wanted to sing for us. He took the score, and just as he was about to sing the first note, he doubled over. His head fell against his chest, and stayed that way.'

"And that's what went down on record. But deep in my heart, down where we all still have a little honesty, where we judge ourselves without mercy, without making excuses, I could never abide by those 'facts.' In our magnificent mise–en–scène, we'd committed one notable error: my accomplice had planted the musical score upside down . . ."

The coachman began to brood after this, as if truly upset. A moment later he touched my hand and said: "We're there! See you tomorrow! Time to get down."

To live is the victory of the fetus. Being born is its only end. During its nine months of reflection, death doesn't seem at all the tragedy the Christian philosophers make of it. One doesn't think in the waiting room. For the fetus, just seeing the light is a triumph. It's everything. Think how long it's had to avoid the machinations of abortion, its various run-ins with all those methods enumerated by the penal code as excuses for depriving a citizen of her civil rights: the freezing shower to make the ovaries shiver; later, the crude, perfumed infusion; and then, later still, when it's clear there's no hope, the probing iron in some menopausal matron's hand, wielded with all the skill of a novice butcher or an ever-so-proper gentleman who considers it quite enough to expectorate *near* the spittoon, so as not to offend passersby. But in the end, at last, the fetus, triumphant, can exclaim: *Toute la lyre!*

Thus, despite its notable success, the face of a newborn reveals something about the precariousness of our life on earth. The womb was an uninterrupted series of threats. The triumph of the fetus can never be more than melancholy; see its wide forehead, as though its tiny frontal lobe has already begun to consider, despite itself, the likelihood of its eventual death by stroke . . .

I hate the great boulevards invented by Haussmann. The people who toil and bore themselves to exhaustion along those streets remind me of the words of Saint Paul: "the wages of sin is death." Yes, they are the whited sepulchers: gorgeous women who flit through life like butterflies, uncertain of whether there's any beauty under their makeup; men who've prolonged their stay in their mothers' wombs by way of these gorgeous women, continuing to live off their maternal blood and pus; wrongheaded men who bend down to retrieve a tiny piece of green paper in case it might have a coin inside, or perhaps an entire fortune; and then, getting in these transients' ways, a waiter who comes out carrying a flowerpot by its handles and places it on the edge of the sidewalk, as though this were the road to Damascus . . .

Nothing spreads sadness like popularity. It knows how to make us bitter, how to cause the same resentment that oppresses us after possessing a woman. Popularity is this: to take a woman into your arms, to feel pleasure approaching, and then, the very next instant, after a brief rest, to have your umbilical cord cut all over again, and find yourself once more with the sadness of a newborn—with their wide foreheads, rheumy eyes, grimaces of pain, wrinkled genitalia. I've experienced popularity, as I think I've already mentioned. I've been quite proud of myself ever since I was a small child, after having discovered no less than five cadavers in the sluice gates of our mill.

That's how precocious children get old before their time. Seven-year-old violin prodigies are old by twenty. All the applause tires out their souls. They get increasingly effeminate. By the age of thirteen, their managers have to work hard to keep their protégés' curls looking properly childish. Beards are plucked. At night, women come to kiss these children like they're sheep— and men come to kiss them like they're women. Such prodigies know all the pleasures but the sensual ones; their childhoods must be eternal. Once they've served out their contracts, they're left to the tender mercies of critics, those deflowerers of knowledge, who put up one makeshift dam after another, hoping to keep any freak floods of intelligence from getting too rapidly disseminated . . . By sixteen, the once precocious child resembles a wealthy fifty-five-year-old businessman, valuing nothing more than pleasure now, surrendering himself without compunction to common soldiers in their fortifications and the peasants who ride the cargo wagons at night, rolling down dead roads.

Even the greatest skeptic can nonetheless catch a glimpse of happiness in a woman's smile . . . happiness, which, as the Arabs say, treads upon golden heels. I knew, as a child, a woman whose look had a certain sweetness to it. Her beauty came from her being nearsighted.

I used to pass by a house where a few of my female relatives lived. At the time, they'd given shelter to an orphan girl who'd committed a terrible sin: well, she'd gone to bed with a man . . .

I've never seen the pain of innocence so intensely reflected in a human eye. Maria Luisa, the orphan, looked at me as one might a passing angel. I was the only man who ever came into her new home since her fatal fall. She'd already spent a week in the darkness of the attic with nothing to eat or drink but hard bread and water mixed with soap, as a punishment for her weakness. My aunts were rigorous moralists—spinsters.

Into this improvised convent came Maria Luisa's Fairy God-mother, hoping to rescue her, and taking on, for this purpose, the form of tuberculosis—saying: "Your deliverance is at hand." This lady who herself looked at me with the eyes of an angel en route to heaven, this woman who'd aspired to the grand title of "mother"—like the little girls who stick pillows under their skirts and say they're pregnant—died at dawn in the care of my religious aunts, who were "certain" that this was for the best. When it was over, they sighed with relief. "God's will has been done," my Aunt Javiera said, whose breasts had never grown and who wore grayish housecoats that pleated in a puff over her chest.

L iving in our needle hole of the Seine valley, near the river, by its endless flow, where the wind often pulls trees up by their roots and the sun roasts the fishermen's skin; by that road unencumbered by any city, along those routes where tramps still chew over their songs of revolution, I've never felt the guiding hand of authority, nor the least hint of a hierarchy controlling my life. My solitude has never had any confidant save my own instincts. Today, however, having joined the rest of the world in that courtyard outside the army fort, I've suffered in a way none of my comrades can comprehend. They just complain about the discipline—and they have no trouble finding the words to complain. I can't find the words. I swallow my pain. There is only one way I can think of to sublimate this experience. Vengeance. Together with my friend here, who speaks in a low, earnest voice, I'd like to scream out my horror at the way men destroy all the beauty in the world by killing children.

I sing my childhood in these pages that no one will ever read since they are written only for me. Nobody ever gave me toys to sap away my manhood, to teach me to be docile and, sadder still, simply ordinary. No. I've never had the tinplate and cardboard gendarmes children play with in the city. Justice is a painted gendarme whose colors rub off in our hands. A gendarme that's been painted, carved, encrusted in the foods we ingest. The trademark of our moribund society, of a nation unhinged, of men who don't know how to hold on to the elegance they possessed as children, when *man*—that obese monster—happily slept.

I was a good geometry student. I loved straight lines. Perpendicular ones above all. These are lifelines, I told myself.

I never stopped to look at the lithograph of the Tower of Pisa that hung in our foyer. Its leaning troubled me. I could see it falling. In the paper each day, I looked for news from Italy first. No, it still hadn't fallen.

But when? My nightmares took full advantage of my concern. The Tower of Pisa eroded spectacularly in my dreams.

I always enjoyed news of such disasters. Were there a lot of fatalities? Oh, not that it really mattered how many citizens were crushed under some wall—what are a few deaths compared to the moral serenity its collapse provided to people like myself, who couldn't bear not knowing when it would finally come down? Certainly old neighborhoods have their particular poetry, patina, the imprint of time; but I stay away from neighborhoods where the buildings all lean up against each other at the elbow like old women in nursing homes trying not to topple over. It's not the walls themselves that bother me so much as the stanchions propping them up. They never seem strong enough. Props that aren't absolutely straight give me goose bumps. My hair stands on end. The same thing happens when I see crooked pictures, and it's even worse when it's a landscape painting making use of perspective—a terrible fad I can't forgive bad painters for indulging. This must explain my excessive love for stereoscopes: a perfectly placed line sweetens my soul. In the Bougival cemetery there was once a truncated pyramid that obstructed my view of the main street. I tipped the monument over. Someone righted it and put even more supports around the thing, but I destroyed it again, repeatedly, until the owners of the plot came to realize the gravity of the aesthetic assault they'd perpetrated upon nature and reduced the height of the tomb. I don't know if they also shortened the corpse.

Proportion—the source of all beauty in architecture—was nearly the end of me. Bougival is an attractive town, I suppose, in the context of eighteenth-century architecture, but there's a triumphal arch that the Romans left in Zaghouan which is so stunning that every woman who passes in front of it acquires a beauty frankly terrifying in its perfection. I felt ill before this triumphal arch. They arrested me for desertion, and that arrest was my salvation. Otherwise, I would've died like a voluptuous Buddha there on the roadside, contemplating the poetry that the perfect proportions of those architectural lines showered down upon the women of our day and age—just as it endowed the local women with a similar charm two millennia earlier, those same African women who made a temple out of love, in which they lay themselves down to pray.

Love is the most profound aesthetic experience in a person's life. Faith cannot compete. It and love tend to go their separate ways—though they do often stage reunions on battlefields, taking refuge together, as when they were first born, in men stricken with fear, nothing more than the terrified playthings of God.

Once, men possessed the sea, the mountains, and the stars. They put them to use in their poetry, in their dreams and deaths. Today, however . . .

One can see, sometimes, at a distance, along the basin of the Seine, an imprecise something that, given its lovely surroundings, must, one assumes, be a child or a beautiful woman. As one gets closer to the something, though, one finds instead what should be a rather appealing human being is in fact nothing more than a small dog, a camera, or a bicycle.

The coal merchant's son, Joaquín, had inherited a cuirass—by way of the continual, chaotic game of blackmail and allegiance played by maids and porters. This cuirass wasn't ancient, but rather Republican in origin. As Joaquín kept watch over his father's coal, he entertained himself by adjusting this body armor. Imagine the darkness of the coal pit, and that dirty-faced child encased beneath a breastplate of steel—it's nothing less than the evocation of a vanished era. No historian could have conceived of a more perfect scene, entirely of a piece: Joaquín, beneath his mesh and plating, as an antique warrior, a statue of Mars hidden beneath the earth, awaiting the shovel that would bring him to light.

As Joaquín couldn't hide his contentment at feeling himself prisoner in his steel corselet, I became quite jealous, wanting to feel the embrace of something similar . . . I couldn't buy a cuirass, no matter how I dreamed of one. So I bought a stiff corset the color of sailcloth instead, and learned then the secret delectation women must feel as they are silently, constantly, shaped.

I'd discovered the sheath of voluptuousness. The Shulamith lying upon Solomon would have no other objective: my corset put pressure upon those same nerve clusters that gave me so much pleasure when alone . . .

Mention of Joaquín has brought me to my child-hood again. Is this the so-called "blue hour"? Who named it that? There is always a certain sarcasm in people who live within the limits of the law, but were once little delinquents . . .

A man approached me one day on my way home from school. I was polite as a little girl whose schoolmistress lavishes her with the sort of caresses that would drive an older person wild with delight.

"Do you know where someone could rent a house around here?" he asked.

"There, across the street," I said.

"Why don't you go pick up the keys for me so we can take a look?" he asked.

I went to get them and we entered the un-rented house. The doors to all the rooms were open and our footsteps made their way to the center of the building. At the top of the stairs, the friendly man who'd made me his associate gave me some caramels with one hand and with his other unbuttoned my pants.

"How pretty it is," he said with the forthright smile of a savage, caressing me.

I heard someone calling to me. A distant voice I hadn't heard since my mother died. Where did it come from? I moved back down the stairs like an automaton. I went toward the voice. The friendly man followed me, and when I'd gotten farther away, running now, trying to make up for the time I'd lost, I saw him close the door diligently behind me, looking at me much as a poor poet might, peeking into the Ministry of Finance.*

---

* The Editors would like to state their objection to the exploitative tabloid style here employed by Monsieur le Vicomte de Lascano Tegui. (*Note in the first edition.*)

I still didn't know what love was. When I approached little girls at school, the natural female scent that emanated from their skin, and which—whenever they noticed it themselves—made them blush, gave me the same vertigo I'd experience later at the nearness of a woman's breast. The mere aroma of those little girls elevated me to the same delectable heights of emotion that the curves of the bodies of passing women would arouse in me as I matured. For instance, the crisis of sensation when a neighbor named Julia asked me to come up and see her one day. She was a widow. She sat me on her lap and kissed my sex. Julia was my first lover. She took me by the hand with all her thirty-five years of experience. She took a great interest in me.

A spiritualist, she believed staying in Bougival was a way to stay close to the spirit of her husband, who'd drowned in the

Seine. Having found over twenty corpses in the sluice gates of the mill by this time, the whole village saw me as one of its favorite sons. A funeral business gave me a hundred business cards to slip into the pockets of the drowned. The family of the deceased always took the hint. The funeral home gave me ten francs for each new client I secured for them. The widow Julia couldn't escape the spreading oil slick of my fame. The body of her husband had never been found. Would I be the one to find it? Not yet—and in the meanwhile, she couldn't remarry. Without a corpse, there was no way to verify her bereavement. Since I couldn't find him for her, she was obliged to solicit a divorce on the grounds that she'd been abandoned. On the eve of the court's decision, in the presence of a medium, she called up her wandering husband. The medium declared she saw the man's spirit just behind me, above my head, and he was holding a poster with the words:

An eagle eats a banana,
and all of humanity is golden.

The medium, who was a mason's wife, interpreted the enigmatic poster as follows:

"Eagle: pride. Banana: perfume. Humanity: warm blood. Gold: fleeting happiness."

We sat in mournful silence as though we'd understood.

I wanted to live my own life. I was fourteen then, which explains my anxiety. A great desire to get as far away as possible dragged me through the streets until nightfall. How would I get home? The spectacle of the countryside always swept me away with it, without objection. At that age, I read adventure books about distant savage continents. How I loved those islands supposedly towed by the dragons of the Middle Ages. Sadly, those islands no longer existed. How I wanted to go into combat with the ferocious natives and wildlife of unexplored lands! They were incomplete beings, above whom floated the arrogant superiority of a boy from civilization.

I knew Stanley's travel diaries by heart. I read and recited them to the other children in Bougival. The majority of those kids are street toughs now. But what is the *apache* if not a hunter of wild beasts born into the wrong age?

Having read those books, I saw the world as divided into two hemispheres: the hemisphere of stabbing, and then the far more prestigious hemisphere of shooting.

And I had a photograph of myself taken with a revolver in my hand.

She was the daughter of an alcoholic. Her father had very white hands, the hands of someone who'd never done a day's work, and the girl grew up admiring them. At seven years old, she fell in love with a woman who'd touched her hair as she passed. Why? Because the woman had beautiful hands. This was the girl's only desire. That stranger's hands had brought her all the sensations of beauty. She was poor and lived alone and never dreamed as a farm-boy does of setting fire to haystacks just to enjoy the magnificence of their burning over the fields at night. But men alone can't always be the vehicle for all the beauty in one's life. Pity the woman who gives herself to a man just because he has curly hair or straight! . . . Thus does she forsake paradise all over again.

One day, her father called to Gabriela, whom we called Mademoiselle Fifí among ourselves. She watched the luminous trail of her father's hands as they picked up a pocket knife. This movement made his hands even more beautiful than usual, and, taking hold of his penis, he cut it off in front of her. Blood covered his hands as they deposited his organ on the kitchen table. Gabriela lost her mind after that. Still, she was a generous madwoman. She'd offer herself under bridges, in doorways at dusk, between empty stalls in the market. While I took her, she'd lick my hands. As our union ended, her saliva would get thick and foamy like the spit that collects on the bits of runaway horses.

I've watched my family fall the way a leper watches his cold, swollen hands drop off in pieces. My poor parents got old and died.

My father brought back a crocodile from the Amazon; we kept it in a pool covered with wire netting. The crocodile slept for several months and in that time swarms of horseflies and mosquitoes took up residence on his craggy back. They contracted his sleeping sickness from drinking his blood. When the crocodile showed any signs of life, it was almost always on the same side of his body: he'd open the eye along that coast and watch us sadly. He was still tired. The noise from the street, the vibration of carts loaded with beans and potatoes, simply fueled his nightmares. And then, on one of those days when the crocodile opened its eye, a mosquito managed to escape the general lethargy and bit my younger brother, who liked to run his finger along the extensive teeth of our visitor—and thanks to this chance bite, my brother experienced the inexpressible pleasure of serving as a medical experiment. He died of tiredness.

My brother was buried in the lowest, dampest part of the cemetery. The Seine flooded it in winter, when the waters rose. Between the mud and mire, we recovered the cross the current had carried some distance away. The grave itself seemed to have tried to follow its marker, dragging itself along the riverbed, as if that pine box with lead handles no longer contained my brother's fleshless bones, but simply the divine and Egyptian soul of our sacred crocodile.

They say the gondoliers of Venice are the most agile men on earth. Anyway, of that part of the earth perpetually in motion. I've never seen them, but I imagine them to be like black cats, the most agile animals I can think of. If ever a stranger made a real impression on an hour of my life—those hours that have floated by like reflections of clouds—it was the stokers working the steam barges going down the Seine. I've seen those stokers up close, leaning on the rails of their ships, weary as Childe Harold, watching the world pass, unmoved by the gray, protean smoke escaping their stacks. Only their eyes have life to them. Pariahs living so close to fire and under mounds of coal, their red pupils were ringed by halos of black dust caught in their long lashes—lashes made beautiful by this carbon: the almond eyes of fabulous, exotic queens. The beauty of their eyes moved me—as Antinous was struck by the eyes of one of Hadrian's legionnaires.

I've known the frissons caused by the mysterious, the hermetic, the Oriental. Eyes that seem to contain in themselves the achievement of all the unspeakable aspirations of our latest literary trends. These were travelers to strange lands—romantic eyes. Fixed in the landscape for an hour, they became suggestive, terrifying, and beautiful, like the eyes in paintings along the dark hall of some damp castle; enormous and fascinating, like the painted eyes of mummies, like the elongated eyes of Egyptians . . .

I've felt those fatal eyes look upon my boyish—perhaps occasionally girlish—soul. Eyes encrusted in the stokers' faces—Greek statues during the decline had eyes made of agate, emerald, and gold. Those eyes passed by, mirroring me without seeing me, vacant of all sense or sentiment. Eyes the same as the cheap crystal eyes of embalmed animals in provincial museums.

Marie Germain changed genders at twenty-two years of age. I established mine when I was only ten, an age when boys flirt with the idea of being female and some are already as sensitive as girls. I had a classmate we all kissed as if he weren't another boy. And Osvaldo—that was his name—was thrilled with all of this attention, because he didn't catch on that we were courting him, and that this was why we all offered him the best of ourselves. We used to invite him to take walks with us, and he gave us the added pleasure of having to lie to his parents in order to come along: he would sneak out of his house to join us. The skin on his face and legs was entirely feminine, and I was so jealous that I ended up having a falling out with him. I almost preferred to abstain from his company entirely than watch him belong equally to all my friends.

When we eventually made up, I no longer took any pleasure in him. He repulsed me. Osvaldo, as a result, would do anything to make me like him again. I'd take him to the riverbank and make him trap leeches for me: I'd tell him to go barefoot into the underbrush along the riverbank and he'd come out with leeches fastened to his calves. As he helped me with my leech business (and he'd kiss me ardently as I exploited him—I couldn't stand it), he got thinner, taller, and his rosy complexion turned sallow. One day they expelled him from the Convent of Saint Francis, and after that I only saw him occasionally, in Paris, powdered like a girl and walking on the balls of his feet, looking back to see if there was anyone following him. When he turned his head, he'd smile. A look, one might say, as though he'd just received some sort of sign.

I never found any hints in Bougival's history that the town might once have been a Huguenot stronghold. But where Osvaldo was concerned, my village showed itself to be indignant and Puritan to a fault. It was cruel how the townspeople singled him out. They took great pleasure in offering him up as a sacrifice, making an example of him, imposing a strict, unending policy of *droit du seigneur* upon him in exchange for a fleeting sensual pleasure . . . forcing themselves on that poor, sick boy, who was as fit for the sanatorium as he was innocent before the law. After all, what wouldn't he do for us so long as we went on keeping him company? As a child, Osvaldo had bored peepholes in the doors to his mother's and sister's rooms—the former had now married for the second time, the latter was a fifteen-year-old virgin with a luscious Spanish body. The perverts who liked to accompany Osvaldo on his viewings could choose whichever hole they preferred: the one that looked in on Osvaldo's libertine stepfather, or the one that opened onto the rosy, naked innocence of the young virgin sitting at her mirror, feeling the anxiety common to every lonely woman during the infinite solitude that is night in the provinces.

At a certain point in my life, I remember having seen and spoken to people who'd achieved a greater degree of perfection than the people I know now. But I've forgotten the details of these encounters . . .

I also remember that, at that age, coach-horses would smile at me. Yes, they smiled at me . . . and leave us not concern ourselves with the incredulity of those men who have never been children, and whose refusal in those days to believe my stories crippled every one of my affirmations with doubt as soon as they left my mouth.

Fish—I refer to the ones in the Seine—are old and tired by the time they arrive in Bougival. They are experts in all the varied methodologies of the art of fishing. When I whistle to myself on the riverbanks, I see fish entertaining themselves by flipping out of the water to enjoy my music. This when they won't move so much as an inch for a bit of bait on a line. Because fisherman who don't know how to whistle are boring.

NOVEMBER 2, 18—

Raimundo the coachman invited me back up onto his coachbox. Once again came the stories of the neighborhood, one after another, because he still likes to keep a little of the confessional in his life. We were riding around the green bonnet of Mont Valérien when we saw a large cluster of young women watched over by two nuns. Raimundo warned me:

"Look at the girls, kid, at every one—you need to get used to them. Any man who lets a girl pass unobserved will end up with an enemy at his back. You have to look at them, adore them, value them—some shamelessly, some sadly, but don't let any woman be an exception. Nature won't forgive you for it."

Raimundo the coachman then looked over at the nuns—as though through an open fly.

He added: "I know them . . . I know them! From the Soeurs de la Charite de Jesus! You know, there once was a nurse from that order who fell in love with a patient—he was one of those invalids who feel more at home in hospitals than out in the world, and she really was dying of love for what was left of that wretched, suffering bit of humanity . . . just the sort of thing city men like to hear, since they hope to get the same treatment when their turns come. Hers was a love without limits, you know, spiritual, and watching her patient through the windowed door of his room, the nurse ran her eyes over the sweet line of the man's profile just as death began to tug at it. A love without words! But death, who's also a woman, got jealous: it became a battle between two women, you see, and death soon got the upper hand by poisoning the nurse's drinking water with an aphrodisiac . . . her love went from purely spiritual to carnal to the point of paroxysm! Alone in her quarters, the nurse descended to the basest depths of earthly love. Death had won. The devout woman died in grand fashion. They buried her with all the pomp reserved for those who die in the line of duty. A tricolor flag covered her coffin. The other nurses, doctors, and convalescents accompanied her remains to their final rest. A carpenter's apprentice who'd gone to find the hospital door behind which the nurse had expired followed the beautiful procession with the entire doorframe on his shoulder—a new Simon of Cyrene. However, the door he carried had been infected with the late sister's lust, and thus a new fount of love emerged on the earth . . ."

Bougival is full of old women. Their big faces fill the windowpanes. My God, how old they are! Not even death can get their attention. They'll only die once they finally tire of listening to the ringing of the village bells.

It's the same story with the hens of Bougival. Unlike our roosters, they never seem to make any progress toward the chopping block. Not even when they change owners. On the contrary: if stolen, the thief simply ends up taking them to market, and they go on living. It's as though, without admitting it, man and bird have come to an agreement—an agreement that would be much more precise if humans didn't despise their fellow creatures so much; if, instead of wasting time deciphering ancient Chaldean, we worried a little more about deciphering the language of the animals we actually spend our time with! In any case, I've discovered numerous curious cohabitations in my town—intimate, embarrassing dramas. Now that I've strayed onto this subject, I might as well record the influence that one of my neighbors exercised over the birds in her poultry yard.

My neighbor frequently picked up her hens and chastised them, ridiculously, waggling her index finger: "If anyone comes to steal you, you'd better get away! Don't let yourself be taken away by who-knows-what sort of brute!"

Then she'd let them go, only to return later and repeat her instructions to them one by one.

It is believed that the birds understood.

Her hens were the most anxious chickens I've ever seen. The slightest sound would send them scurrying; they'd run, horrified, to take refuge under their owner's skirts.

Perhaps this seems charming to you? But statistics show that there's always an increase in instances of heart disease in populations living under a tyrannical regime. Those hens, under the pressure of their owner's constant threats, all died young—suffocated by disproportionately small hearts, certainly worth less than the livers of geese from Périgueux . . .

T he world," the coachman told me, "is slowly committing suicide . . ." He paused to think of a way to illustrate his point, setting aside his whip, and then added:
"For example, every single day the semen of our great ge-niuses—that most vital of fluids—leaks out through an opening that is directly connected to their spinal columns, and so they are gradually reduced to nothing—those same arrogant geniuses who, if they were allowed to develop fully, would, admittedly, prove quite a nuisance to humanity . . . but who are also our only means of moving forward! This is the trade-off we make in the modern age . . . perhaps solitary vice should be considered the social virtue *par excellence*! Certainly if people made love on the streets, in front of everyone, health and hygiene levels in the city would be above reproach. Onanism, however, despite

putting an end to so much human progress, has the advantage of culling our herd, and of uniting those of us who are left! It's an elimination test.

"For ages it's proven impossible to unite all the strata of mankind. Our geniuses were pretentious and individualist and unapologetically so. Their destiny was to lead all other men to the slaughter and thus be left alone in their brilliance, solitary and lofty as the mountains. But see, masturbation has put an end to those demigods. They couldn't survive the modern world without masturbation. In other words, they've become "civilized." Women—in whom, you know, all the capital sins are combined: everywhere to be seen, nowadays, but now not quite so accessible as in the days of kings and tyrants—breezed gently through the eyes of our geniuses and lay down upon the soft cushions of their cerebellums . . . Yes, masturbation took over, making these geniuses descend to the common territory of all base mortals—tarnished now, despite their greatness! Now they look like gray stone military monuments: tall, and with a primitive, corrupt sort of authority about them—but entirely anti-aesthetic. They lie in wait for us at night, their stony bodies obstructing the paths of all things tender, soft, and beautiful—hoping to trip us up, petrified and perverse! That's their revenge, you see, upon the rest of us! And that's precisely what they've told me, when I've taken their confessions—when I managed at last to work their souls free from their calcified bodies, the same way you peel the hide off a slaughtered cow . . . brute force."

At twenty, she was an artist's girlfriend. She didn't deserve the distinction. She lacked enthusiasm. She interrupted his work with the same misplaced solemnity that led her to sleep with him on a rainy day just to avoid getting her feet wet and then move to Bougival and open a flower shop. In Bougival, her shop was considered a useless luxury. As she sat waiting for customers, the hours passed and her daughter grew. The artist sent her eighty francs a month to show he still remembered her. She divided up the francs with myopic delight into four weekly sums. The old florist would go to the post office every Tuesday to cash her money order. Her daughter was in charge when she was out, and so planned Tuesday dates with one boy or another. That's how we, the boys of the town, found out Anita had a rash on her back. She was saving up for her future by acquiring gifts from admirers who came to see her rash. One gift she liked in particular was an ornamental comb that cost fifteen francs. At last, Anita disappeared without saying good-bye. Her mother only noticed her absence on a Tuesday, when she realized there was no one to watch the store. She became timid and stopped going out. She made the mailman cash her money orders for her and bring by her twenty weekly francs directly to the shop. Without air and sunshine her plants all dried up.

Novelists overplay their hands when they put an end to their characters with some catastrophe—a terrible fire, a murder, what have you. They don't trust in the asphyxiating monotony of everyday life. The florist's was no more fascinating than a piece of dried seaweed. What she owned, where she lived, her days and nights: all were of the same homogenous consistency, bringing to mind the dull, lifeless backgrounds of the sepia landscapes commonly produced by professional photographers.

The children of degenerates step into life before other children. They start living centuries earlier. Health means nothing more than living in normal time. A broken watch ticks more often than one in perfect condition. It lives more. The children of the abnormal are mortgages owed by their parents. They're born old. Born intelligent to the point of insanity. Sensitive to the point of silence. They've lived in their mothers' bellies, their fathers' blood, for years and years of an exhausting sensuality. They're born with severe and well-worn faces. Their eyes are already jaded, as if they've seen too many Corot landscapes and gray was the only color in their cosmologies. Their hands are worn and they bite at their mothers' breasts when suckling. They're premature lovers. The wise children of the great languishing of our spinal fluids!

This was what made my neighbor's daughter so strange, and destined her to die long before the other skinny girls in Bougival. At a year old, she could already speak with ease. She was given to hyperbole. Things didn't interest her because they existed—only because of the sensation they produced in her. She never picked things up; just passed her hands over them.

Noise bothered her. She listened closely, frightened. She couldn't help but translate noise, in her mind, into intense emotion (if only sailors could do the same when describing storms at sea in their three-hundred page naval manuals . . .). The first words she sounded out were adjectives. They remained her primary mode of communication for as long as she lived. She knew things by their qualities. She called water "cold," she said "sweet" for milk, "hard" for bread—and it was the same with anything pleasant: an apple, her mother, a wooden horse, a silver bucket. For all the things that made her cry, she said "Boo." "Boo" was the catch-all word for all the bad things that haunted the life of this tiny, sensitive girl destined to die on an autumn afternoon, because life couldn't possibly give her what her genius demanded.

She died, incidentally, in my arms the other day, after I took her out onto the balcony and showed her the distant panorama of Paris. On seeing it, the girl, fifteen months old, turned to me and said, as if we were in agreement: "Boo?"

When night comes, crowds hit the old neighborhoods like herds of boars escaping the purest of women (Diana)—clerks twisted and gnawed by their desires till they resemble the old files from their offices, the sex maniacs, vampires, and still-ashamed pederasts, all looking for refuge in the slums and suburbs and peeping into the buildings there, unbuttoning their pants and pissing at random against the walls and trees.

They wait for accomplices who never show up and who they suppose might be disguised as a worker heading home for the day, a bag over his shoulder; a wisp of a girl running errands; or a boy coming home late from school, wrapped in the narrow cape some cheap tailor made as skimpy as possible. The boy's hands are purple from the cold, and the armies of the perverse see these swollen, miserable hands as exotic fruit, the first fruits of a midday harvest.

It was a night I couldn't stay in any chair, felt as restless as an animal driven by instinct, with no fixed destination, wanting the dark alleys and nothing else. I went by the factories that had started to spring up on the boggy Seine flood-lands.

A smell of hay, of manure, brick ovens, and recently discharged chemicals drifted gradually from the shadows. The sun had fallen into the oblivion of the horizon. In front of me rose a giant factory. The street divided it in two. In the opposite direction, climbing the hill where the factories dumped their waste, a man was approaching leading two large white horses in worn halters.

The horseman passed and behind him, hurrying to keep up, was a cross-eyed man with a zinc box on his back.

In a pit, among the garbage heaps, a woman who was really still a girl was poking at the ground. She was burying a biscuit tin containing six playing cards with a pin stuck through them, a piece of lodestone, the hearts of two doves, and a cameo of her seducer.

In that black landscape, she was a happy and religious creature.

C limb on up, kid."

The coachman invited me to sit beside him. He was headed to Nanterre. I didn't feel like talking. So we just rode quietly. Knowing I'd climbed up onto his coachbox for a reason, he said, "Only alcohol contains true happiness. The rest, little boy, isn't worth a gobbet of spit. It's pure waste, empty debauchery. Do you know Marie Roger?"

I nodded like I was trying to remember.

"Your neighbor Marie, Nicholas the shoemaker's wife."

"Yes," I said.

"She sent for me this morning. I thought she maybe wanted me to pick up a package for her in Paris.

"'Monsieur Raimundo,' she said, sounding very distressed. 'Nicholas has gone crazy!'

"'Crazy?'

"'I sent for you so you could take him to Paris.'

"To a hospital in Paris is what I thought. And as one has to do on such occasions, I went to get my coach. We barely managed to get Monsieur Nicholas to climb in. He didn't recognize us. When I told him we were going to Paris to see his brother, though, he agreed to come along.

"The poor guy was really mad—mad in every possible way.

"Along the way, Monsieur Nicholas, who didn't recognize me, got down to say hello to various people we passed . . . And when I asked Madame María what street we were headed to, she said: 'Go wherever you want.'

"I was baffled. So now maybe she'd gone mad as well?

"'For example, we could go to the pont de Solférino if you'd like,' she said. So we went. There were a few benches on the bank. Monsieur Nicholas got down, then Madame María after him and her daughter, who'd come along with us. They put him between them and asked me to wait down the street. When I pulled away, they went over to some gendarmes sleeping against a wall of the Tuilieries Garden. I saw them point to husband and father and make a gesture to explain he was crazy. The gendarmes came over.

"'Do you know him?' one of them asked the two women.

"'No,' they replied in unison. 'We just happened to pass by and noticed he was out of his mind. It's dangerous to just leave him here. Whoever he is, he needs to be taken to an asylum.'

"Monsieur Nicholas smiled as if he was grateful for this attention and so the two gendarmes called to a passing cab and took this lunatic—without any known family—to a public asylum . . .

"And thus it was that Marie Roger and her daughter rid themselves of a lunatic. The state took custody of him until he died. The family didn't have to pay a thing. And since Marie Roger couldn't rid herself of his shoe store with the same ease, it still belongs to her . . .

"So, do you see how everything on the earth is just waste and debauchery? Good thing we can rely on a glass of something or other from time to time to help shield our eyes from it all . . .

"Now, kid, climb down—and before you say good-bye, I'm going to treat you to a dose of holy water."

He filled a glass with absinthe and said a blessing over it with all the unctuousness of an old priest—not to mention the expansive sloppiness of a dockworker. His voice, like that of Saint Julian, had the timber of a bronze bell.

W hen the mayor's son left his house, all of us other boys flocked together the way small dogs scurry around each other whenever a big mastiff goes by. We felt an enormous respect for this boy who went to school in Paris and had already earned, at thirteen years of age, the honor of being called out to from the brothel window . . .

Nobody, no full-grown woman, has ever affected me, in all her voluptuousness, as much as that eleven-year-old girl who had the forty-year-old eyes of her mother and the voluptuous body movements of an aunt of hers who visited Bougival every Monday and dressed in loud, gaudy colors. How many women have I squeezed out like lemons and tossed away. I've spurned even the most intriguing, same as all the rest. Only the memory of that neighbor of mine—a girl who even then was as impalpable as a memory—still persists in the solitude of my ennui and despair. She's the fairy godmother of my entire sensibility. My imagination can't help but fly like a sharp, swift arrow toward that moment when her female intuition made her set one of her feet on a cornerstone and show me the length of her other leg. No other woman, no experience with any of my other coy mistresses ever matched the brilliance of that girl's single movement, that girl who didn't need to raise her leg but did nonetheless, showing me the creamy rose color of it, knowing somehow—born sensitive to such niceties because of her gender—that she'd thereby made herself the most precious fortune I'd ever possess.

I would soon have to rejoin my regiment. Yet, how could I leave behind that beauty in flower, that fugitive dove, who added to her beauty and youth the luscious blossom of inno- cence, brought to bloom by instinct, that tragic gardener?

We were neighbors. On the eve of my departure, in my bed each morning, I'd hear her leaving for school and my ears would take in the deliciousness of her movements. I could pick out the sound of one of her breasts as it shifted away from its twin, both too large for her tiny frame—a sound that, as Barbey d'Aurevilly said of a virgin in Memling, resolved the question of the immaculate conception for me long before the Church ever would . . .

In families that fall into bankruptcy, there's usually some foreigner who marries into the family and soon finds himself supporting the entire household. Likewise, it's always the aunts and uncles who are the legitimate moral foundations of a family, not one's parents. Generally spinsters and bachelors, these aunts and uncles are the confidants of their nieces and nephews—the true parents of their souls. True, some of these aunts and uncles vegetate like furniture in the recesses of the family home, but it's the ones who disappear, the adventurers, who seem the most prestigious: Before we, as children, can get a sense of them, they leave. They float in the fog of the past. We grow up admiring them—without admitting it—because these magical figures have the ability to open the gates to a fabulous orchard of fantasy . . . Some were gallant, others depraved, but still—each possessed of their own peculiar genius, even the ones who were womanizers, syphilitic and suspect, the Don Juans of their times. I had an uncle who disappeared in the troubles of '48. He was the most beautiful of my grandmother's six children—and she only spent two thirds of our fortune on him. Sensuous like all first-borns, a love child, he took off for the revolution of '48 with the confidence of someone heading out on an assignation. A woman came around to see him the night before. That was the last we heard of him.

One more twilight. Sadness fills my soul and my thoughts are all of you. It's seven in the evening. Right now you're getting on the train. The other travelers are following you with their eyes. Oh, if I could only forget! Will it destroy me? No. You're just a long shadow that's crossed my life. I won't see you again. I know it. The eyes that loved you have lost their quicksilver. So much effort! I'm out of hope and sorry because you remain incomplete. No other chance lover will ever have the same audacity, will ever be able to break through your crystal coffin and touch you, wake you, free you from your spell. But don't worry. I'm like Pyrrhus after his victory. I've understood my defeat.

As I sink to the depths this evening, like something trapped in an aquarium, there's nothing in all this blue but the thought of you. Your perfume wafts in and evokes the doves we heard flying over our sunrises, from our shared room in Beautiran. Do you remember how the doves that flew past our window seemed to be fanning us, flapping only one wing?

This page is inexplicable in the diary of my life. I've written it tenderly, as though I was once in love. It seems like sacrilege to include it as part of this intimate experiment, in which we're testing the consolatory effects of speaking badly about others to ourselves.

They called her La Española. I met her when she was already old, tall, clumsy. In the days of the Empress Eugénie, she came all the way to Bougival for an audience with La Española. A vague kinship connected them. La Española was even invited to stay in the Emperor's home, on occasion.

She was the one who predicted my mother's death. She spread her tarot cards across our table, in the shape of the Maltese cross. But she didn't tell people's fortunes for money. No; hers was a higher calling. In the south of Spain, where she was born, the locals had apparently inherited numerous ailments from their old Arab conquerors; but, in addition, they'd also inherited various means of curing them—generally by touch. While the university was still claiming that cataracts were incurable, this Señora de Salvadores triumphed as an ophthalmologist—cataracts were her specialty. (You may have heard that there are sixty or so legal classifications for blacks in the United States; in much the same way, there are many subtle distinctions separating one form of blindness from another.) Señora de Salvadores's hands had a gift for moving gently over one's eyes without causing the least discomfort or damage. She cured cataracts, dispersing those clouds by rubbing, by sanding them down.

The only tool she employed, aside from her fingers, was a souvenir from her days of fortune and youth: she had ground down the mother-of-pearl ribs of the decorated fans she'd used to flirt with back in the bullrings of Andalusia, and would dump this abrasive substance over the afflicted corneas, sanding down the opaque layers of cataract until she could simply remove the remnant by touch. Then she'd rub an eyelash under the affected area.

Each of Señora de Salvadores's fingernails shone with a black patina, and during her procedures she'd wear fingerless, black lace gloves, their light-pink silk ribbons tied around her wrists.

He boarded the train just as it started to depart. He sat in front of me and his initial glance enveloped me in such an atmosphere of confusion that I couldn't free myself from it until he disembarked.

Tall, blond, reserved, he was very self-possessed. His every move seemed to slide over an invisible layer of velvet. There was no more of a sound when he moved his arms than when his eyes moved under their lashes. Was I bewitched? The more attractive he became, the more I suffered. I couldn't escape his obvious pedigree. Over the course of our trip, his eyes seemed to get closer to mine, his lips begin to unfurl. Did he want to talk to me? This state of continual indecision went on until I felt tied to the spot and restless. I wanted to break free of the threads restraining me. I wanted to yell. But somehow, luckily,

I restrained myself . . . I felt it wouldn't have made the least dif-
ference to shout: my words would have turned out irrelevant,
emasculated, and my voice would have come out thin and reedy
like a girl's. The man was perturbing me to the point of anguish.
At last, nervous lest someone hear the feminine voice trembling
in my throat, I lowered my eyes. I needed to get away from the
manly power of that adorable, elegant creature. This was an un-
sustainable situation. At last I raised my eyes from their atone-
ment and saw him looking at my hands, saw how, from his perspective, they must appear so soft and pink, how my lips were
so red as to seem painted, how my clothes were of blue silk and
my cuffs and collar made of lace. This was the inexplicable state
in which I spent the rest of the trip.

His lips unfurling, wanting to speak; his eyes moving closer
and closer to mine, wanting to understand me. His hands barely
moved. The wind hardly ruffled his hair as it whipped through
the drafty car. And when he got ready to leave, giving a last lin-
gering look over my person, I watched him pack away the potion,
the perfume, the mist that had overpowered me—snatching it
up with a jealous flick of his wrist.

There are intellects notable for their prodigious memory and then others simply inspired by the great chaos of the imagination. My own superiority stems from nothing so much as my own powers of observation. I'm a product of myself. I've seen the world through the poor little prism of my eyes. No, I never made use of borrowed eyes. And that's why it was—through observation, a reflexive way of looking—that I always kept myself at a distance from my friends, kept aloof from my teachers. I deduced, for example, by meticulous observation, that a boy from my village was going to turn out to be a homosexual—nature simply wanted it this way. Nature hadn't, early on, been able to make up its mind as to whether or not he should have been conceived in the first place. Then he was born a month early. The whole world fawned over him, and his father bounced him on his knee so often as to displace his proper, masculine sense of pleasure, until it came to reside deep in his rectum, silently contributing to his deviance. As a joke, I would caress the nape of his neck, stimulating without meaning to, the activity of his medulla; the girls kissed him as they would another woman and his voice stayed crystalline and his eyes infantile, melancholy, and (why?) loving. His thumbs became deformed like the thumbs of those degenerates who do nothing but abuse themselves day and night. Have you ever seen anything quite so blunt yet unreliable as the thumbs of a sodomite? Next to the rest of their dapper, delicate hands, their thumbs stand out like bastards . . .

They should really only have four fingers on each hand.

Why do I like women whose faces have something of the bony facial structure of sheep?

Is it perhaps because of my distant love for a shepherd, who himself found nothing more beautiful than his animals and the constellation of Aries?

Or because one of my ancestors died on the top of an ancient wall when that wall succumbed to the continuous assault of Roman battering rams?

Because Watteau painted one of my grandmothers, who was incredibly beautiful, with a lamb in her arms?

Because the first religious icon I received was the baptism of Jesus by John the Baptist with the Agnus Dei serving as witness?

Because women with a curled upper lip have something innocent about them?

Because of all this, perhaps . . . and because women with long, almond eyes are irremediably sensual.

One of my school friends was named Gaston. He was one of those strange kids who, conditioned by their upbringing, eventually manage to accomplish something that seems quite extraordinary, given their circumstances—but which is really just the silent culmination of all the lessons they've naturally come by. There are some books children read before they've learned the alphabet; Gaston was already an old man when he was a boy. Or, better, as his childhood was intense and grim, one might compare it to the years between a man's twenty-nine and thirty-fifth birthdays—the approach of middle age. While other children slept under cotton sheets, sheltered from the weather under their lace and swaddling clothes, Gaston spent those same hours out in the elements, in the snow, in the sun, in the wind and water. His mother sold flowers. Tied up in a makeshift papoose, he hung from his mother's back as she put together her many bouquets. Hours passed without her thinking about the boy. He was like a stick doll. He cried at first, but his tears didn't have the least effect on his mother—though they did attract plenty of customers. Gaston stopped when he realized that crying was not to his benefit. He just stared. Pupils dilated. He learned to read on his own. Sometimes, it was the red and yellow wheels of the passing cabs that entertained him. Other times, it was the iron gate of a garden. Most of the time, it was his mother's multicolored bunch of flowers in her basket, and then, when she set him down on his stomach, the gutter running level with the line of the sidewalk, dogs, the heels of passersby, the tips of umbrellas, the wooden shoes of municipal street sweepers . . .

It seemed as though he would never grow up, trapped in his diapers, constrained within the perverse sling his mother had devised; at last one of his sisters came to liberate him, afraid he might stay tiny, like some miniature apple tree in a Japanese garden. By then all the sap that had been unable to reach his branches, so to speak, had pooled instead into his eyes: His eyes didn't just observe, they photographed what they saw. Later, at school, he used to entertain us with these images . . .

When you're a child, or a tourist—which is, after all, an infantile mode in which to travel the world—you might on occasion enjoy those tiny novelty kaleidoscopes or telescopes inside of which skillful manufacturers have placed images of the Cologne Cathedral, the Leaning Tower of Pisa, or the Roman Coliseum. We had no need of these in our class, because inside of Gaston's eyes—if we asked—we could see all the dogs, flower baskets, and carriage wheels of his infancy. It was remarkable. But—oh, the logic of nature!—whenever the girls going home from school would pass by, Gaston's eyes, against his will, would fill with images of nothing but those roses, jasmines, and violets for which his tears, in times past, had served as such persuasive salesmen.

The French have the impression that only people who are a little wrong in the head, suspect types, ever leave their homelands for other countries. But it's not true. Quite the opposite.

I had a friend from Bordeaux, an elegant woman, strikingly tall. I thought all women from Bordeaux would be like her. When I went there, I found there was no one there to equal her. None of the natives even reminded me of her.

I went into a brothel one afternoon and met a Belgian woman from Ostend. She had such beautiful breasts that I reserved the entire house in their honor. I made them lock the doors and searched through their business records for the voluptuous history of those perfect breasts: from where could they have come? When I traveled then to Ostend—believing all the women there would have breasts of equal beauty—I found with sadness that not even their fourteen-year-olds were possessed of such ideal apparatuses as those I'd discovered in Paris . . . those I had lost by allowing myself to get caught up with generalizations in a brothel!

The most beautiful woman I believe I've ever met was Danish, but having discovered some white hookworms beneath the skin of her rosy legs, I developed a profound disgust for Denmark and its women. Later, quite by accident, I stood before the naked daughter of a Danish architect, not knowing what part of the planet she was from—she was the second most beautiful woman I think I've met, and this one didn't have worms on any of her important features. It's never a good idea, you see, to generalize.

Other examples. As a student, I went to a brothel in the southern slums of Paris. One of the women I frequented was English. An absolute delight.

What a beautiful little creature!

They called her "The Star of the South." She was famous throughout the city and even into the countryside. Peasants traveled to see her. But are all English women like her?

No, no one in England was the least bit like her.

And then there was the woman who came out for the last dance at the Tuileries. She seemed to have stepped, at once, out of Balzac and some distant French province. She was a dark-skinned queen. Quite poised. The midday sun had ripened her alongside the fields of oranges. Above all she radiated distinction and nobility—blue blood.

I discovered her later in a brothel in Seville: her native city. She was the daughter of a cigar maker.

From this interminable rosary of vexations, I speculate that the best citizens of every country emigrate because they feel slightly superior to their countrymen, able to be quite outstanding individuals without their national context to support them. Each of these, then, are worth as much in themselves as an entire nation. In fact, they are their own nations: nations without geographic roots. They recline upon the clouds, where Zeus set his throne, those clouds that veiled the feet of immortal Hebe.

A nd so the old coachman climbed up onto the coach-box, where I was already installed. It was time to go. I snapped the whip and we were off, me playing coachman and he acting a little out of sorts, as if fallen on hard times, unhappy at now playing the sad role of passenger.

Crossing a street, I almost hit a skinny old man dressed as a gendarme. Just in time, my friend grabbed the reins from me with all the equanimity of the father confessor he'd once been—back when the hymens of his parishioners were in his personal, pious care. In exchange for the pleasure of the reins, which he didn't return, he told me the story of my near-victim, now behind us.

"Back when I was a boy," the coachman said, "that man we just passed by was the forest warden for the Lord of Croissic, though he never really knew how to take advantage of his job. His conscience was always getting in the way—he was too taken with his responsibilities, and then with the memory of a strange incident from his first years on the job. Making his rounds one day, he saw a buck behind some shrubs. He began to move as quietly as he could manage, as though he was a hunter himself and not the supposed protector of his master's game. He let himself be tempted by a catch so beautiful that even his boss would have to approve of his taking a shot. He saw all the many kilos of meat and the pelt he could use later to clean the copper saucepans in his kitchen. He aimed and fired. He heard a cry. His bullet had hit the buck, which toppled over.

"When he went over to retrieve his kill, imagine his surprise when he saw, instead of a buck, a dead poacher. The man's chestnut-colored pants had tricked him.

"A tragedy. And he blamed it all on his imagination. The imagination is what ennobles the savage, you know, and turned our Hottentot grandparents into wise men, kings, and priests. In this man, the poetry of his imagination had led him to commit murder. He was always sorry. And his pain was all the greater because he couldn't now serve as an example to his children of the moral superiority that makes for a happy life. How could he ever be ashamed of their behavior now that he had made himself a criminal?

"For instance, one of his daughters let it be known that she had a lover. How could he counsel his daughter? How give her the moral direction she seemed to lack? Our man, again trusting to his imagination, decided to put on his old uniform and his two decorations—one from helping with a rescue operation and the other honoring twenty-five years of service—the better at least to make a show of *exterior* dignity for the benefit of the wandering sheep he hoped to lead back to the path of righteousness . . .

"But when his daughter finally remembered to come home, her father's high seriousness, the two or three words he saw fit to push around his mouth, only made her straighten her shoulders and march right over to her sister, asking when carnival time was coming, so she could get into worse trouble still.

"With an equal disregard for etiquette," the coachman said, "you almost ran this man over without even noticing his uniform. And if there's some small penalty for hitting a tramp, there are certainly *numerous* penalties for hitting a forest warden—even if it's only a man dressed as a forest warden. The costumes the world makes us put on aren't anything to be ashamed of, you know. No. Clothes should spur our imaginations on, until we bow at last before the radiant creation that is our nation's foremost costume: the king's!"

Women gradually began to replace men in the factory. This is why the women of Bougival began to look so terrible. Particularly the women from the lower-class neighborhoods, whose hair smelled bitter because they were still too fond of the Jewish custom of rubbing almond oil into their hair . . .

It was a factory where they made telephone receivers. At six in the afternoon they closed the shop and the women walked in a line along the Seine. They walked in wooden clogs and sang. They sang, and as they sang they went about in wooden clogs like women from a Greemvaneco, taking great strides.

And I'm going to tell you why they sang. The first shift was of young women between seventeen and twenty years of age. One of them, a friend to all—they always put her in the middle of the line—seemed so delicate that she might break. She was my age. She'd taken an interest in me, and her friends suspected her secret. I always waited for her at a bend in the road. In those days, they didn't sing: I would hear their vulgar laughs approaching, their sour shouts, the cheap ironies of those girls who so often picked fights with one another—their cacophony not unlike the clattering of the machines they had to listen to all day. When they saw me, the workers went quiet. They acted innocent, and only Isabel would look directly at me. The sweet look in her green eyes was as bright as the sunlight falling that same instant. A few meters further down the road, in response to an order that she didn't give, the silence would come to an end, and I'd hear the laughter and jokes once again; then, after some distance . . . she'd turn her head for a last look.

One day she wasn't among her friends, but still feeling the strange power of that fragile girl—destined to die far too early—her friends fell silent as they passed me, same as on all the other days, without the least self-consciousness. Not a single one looked at me. And I knew the truth. Isabel was dying.

Having decided a few days later to inquire about her health, I installed myself again along the bend in the road, where I soon heard a song coming down the way. The women from the factory of supersensitive telephone receivers had replaced their dead friend with a song.

DECEMBER 25, 18—

I shall report to you now a particular moment about which I can be as self-righteous and dishonest as a police informer. The day was sunny and the rumble of a carriage coming along the road hurt my ears. I was thinking about a girl whose enormous eyes, as she blossomed, were the color of green grapes.

I was losing my virginity. I was about to bend down and pick it back up again when I stopped. The indolence that has always given me the indifference of a man in love, that has always set me apart from others, stopped me from bothering.

I went home and only then understood—in the faces of my family—the extent of my loss. I couldn't go back. Who knows where on the path I'd left it; it would be impossible to find. The afternoon was over. A summer storm had blown off the bright canvas of the bohemian circus that had set up shop nearby. A thick, fleeting rain had fallen.

I preferred to distract myself by going to the circus. To watch the lines of the umbrella and the tightrope walker converge—lines that are never entirely perpendicular. To follow a clown through the square where the picadors gather.

I arrived early. The circus hadn't begun its show. As I watched, they lit three lines of gaslights. There were also a few Chinese lanterns at the door and a garland of small oil lamps atop the ticket office.

The band—a bugle, bass drum, clarinet, violin, and triangle—played a waltz. Later they performed a polka.

The triangle marked time. And I saw that the drummer boy had recently attached his triangle to the metal frame of his bass drum with a fresh piece of tendon. Was that, perhaps, my virginity?

DECEMBER 28, 18—

My military service was negligible. I was shuttled back and forth between the barracks at Tunis, Zaghouan, and Sousse, and spent a memorable year in Kairouan. It's a holy city for Arabs, in Africa. A great Saracen wall still surrounds it. Past the train station, progress peters out. The last gasps are in the European neighborhood. There, progress is comprised of a post office, a "Hotel de Francia," and a few brick houses where rent collectors live. Otherwise, the whole neighborhood consists of various isolated multistory houses, which used to remind me—in the shadows of the quick-falling desert dusk—of the wide-mouthed jars in Galard's barbershop, where he kept the leeches that my father used to use once a week.

To this smattering of Europeanism along the edge of the Muslim city's great white wall, we must not forget the local commissary, a town hall, a café with one melancholy pool table, and a brothel—that bastion of order and authority within the world of prostitution.

Doing my service, I met Moreau. He was in the infantry like me. Indifferent to the niceties of military life, we were both just killing time, waiting for our return to Tunis, going back and forth between the Corsican Longobardi's café and Madame Flora's bordello. We felt entirely at home in both places: we took off our jackets in one and our pants in the other. In the café, we played billiards like two boys passing a dull night. At Flora's, the game was to see which of us was more of a man.

My friend Moreau wasn't as tall or strong as I, but nature had endowed him a little more generously than it had me. Oddly, this distinction tended to put a little lead on the wings of his fantasies . . . The women he chose weren't always willing to go with him. They had to get permission from Flora first, who'd come to Africa following in the footsteps of Hercules—she had already presided over a house in Gibraltar. Flora wanted Moreau to herself; he was her private reserve.

In Flora's house, accompanying my friend, the very model of masculine crudeness, I gave, by comparison, the impression of being a somewhat delicate individual, a connoisseur of courtesans, with the air of an urbane man who would never pounce upon his female prey the way coarse farmers dig into a pile of grain to be threshed. This characteristic of mine became even more pronounced later on. But my friend Moreau always arrived at Flora's house of pleasure already drunk. I liked to get drunk while there. The flesh of a woman was a much more intense and penetrating liquor than absinthe. Although I'm ashamed to say it, a beautiful Lorrainese blonde even managed to make me sick with love for her. I wrote poems for her. That is to say, I began constructing my first weapons.

But my verses didn't spring from frustrated dreams and desires. They were the flowers of reality, of satisfaction.

I've managed to learn about other things than pleasure without it costing me too much. For instance: the ennui in brothels is as wide as the Sahara, but a prostitute who gets bored isn't dangerous so long as she loves us—even if her love amounts to nothing more than the fact that she's stopped charging for her time. If, instead, she *gives* us money, the risk begins to grow. In such a case, if we stop visiting her, she's likely not to hesitate to take the opportunity to entertain herself—her solitude and boredom being so great—by writing an anonymous letter and denouncing us to the police. Justice for these women perched on the edge of society's bed is in itself a voluptuous thing. They adore gestures for their own sake, just like the arrogant, momentous language of Racine's tragedies. Not because the protagonists of these tragedies complain a lot, but because they challenge authority and stand up to men the way a thief can stand up to a judge . . .When streetwalkers use irony, it's always before the law. It's their way of getting back at authority figures. I remember overhearing this conversation once:

"Why did you smack the officer who tried to detain you? He'd made a formal accusation of robbery."

"I was drunk."

"That doesn't justify it."

"Look, whenever I end up pregnant or drink a little more than I should, I feel the need to hit a policeman."

Yvonne was my first love. As I said, military service wasn't too heavy a burden. I rarely stayed in the barracks. I don't remember any of my other compatriots. Moreau is the only other soldier I remember from those days when I wasn't required to do much of anything. It was precisely because I had so much leisure time I fell in love—I didn't know what else to do, and that Lorrainese blonde's white skin didn't have a pink or blue base to it, as you'll find in the more commonplace female specimens: a wild salmon, salmon juice was what ran in her veins—so white, with such a white wine inside! Yvonne was a marble cup fit only to be filled by royal slaves and drunk from only by the wealthiest of western tycoons. She soon set up shop in Kairouan on her own; her long-term lover, a brilliant sort of pimp, had put her into business for herself, but she had long since stopped letting him run the show. But, to return to the question of boredom, if a woman who awaits a man in a brothel gets immensely bored, the lover who left her there to do her job in peace will end up dragging the same boredom with him through the streets, plazas, and cafes—as when a gored horse in a bullfight steps on its own intestines. The Lorrainese girl's lover, a dark-skinned man from Marseille, was condemned as we were—much more than we were, in fact—to remain in Kairouan. He slept, drank, wandered about. He was now a representative of that mysterious fraternity of ex-men who justify and preserve the shadows of great cities. And yet this pimp, friendless and disapproved of by all, was nonetheless a fixture in the European neighborhood—as much a fascinating example of Western civilization as one of the rent collectors or the county commissioner. He was the great hope of the local constabulary: they so rarely got to accuse a foreigner of a crime—the foreigners themselves were usually the accusers. This jobless thug was destined to break the law sooner or later. The commissioner waited for him impatiently, in the sadness of his office with its two chairs and one desk, on top of which was a virgin folder meant to contain reports, and then a rubber stamp with which the chief marked his "Letters from the Orient," as Marshal von Moltke called them, writing to his sister while he was in Constantinople.

The Lorrainese girl understood, as a married woman, the delicious risk of our love. For myself, I hoped the commissioner would soon write up a report on this man from Marseille who held my death in his hands . . . Soon enough, an Arab saved me.

A girl far too developed for her age, who knows how or why, always has an agent of the secret police on her tail. The girl serves as the bait that attracts the various satyrs scattered about the city. All the clerks know her. Bureaucrats who've made eunuchs of themselves over twenty years of expediting papers are the usual victims of these boorish policemen. And it's the same for a man with nothing to do: he always has someone on his tail trying to reel him into a pay-by-the-hour motel. One afternoon—as my boredom, like the yawns of the camels grazing by Kairouan, whispered thickly along the courtyard of the Great Mosque—an Arab accosted me. He was one of the guides who showed the city to tourists.

He offered to show me the interior of the Arab world. A Christian can't live among Muslims, but a Christian can see—without it being too much of a sin—Arab women with their faces unveiled. This was the spectacle he offered me. I accepted. Inside the house in question, women were weaving rugs. One of them, a little long in the tooth, berated me in every way she could think of. The other two women, girls really, smiled. When my curiosity was sated, and I headed back out to the street, my guide was waiting for me.

"So?" he asked. I gathered in time that he wasn't curious about my reaction to the interior of the house, which wasn't all that interesting, but instead about the young girls who had smiled at me.

"Very nice, both of them," I told him, without enthusiasm.

"One franc," he responded.

"A franc? What, you want a franc?"

"Yes," he said. "For one franc you can be alone with them for a while, if you like."

I'd never been offered girls so young or so cheap. "So come and get your franc," I said . . . and that's how I met Grisela. The father—because the Arab who'd made this proposal was the father of the two smiling girls—received one franc per expedition, adding up to the significant sum of seven hundred francs in six months . . .

The girl had no time to weave rugs anymore. I hoarded her until the day I returned to Tunis. Grisela's youth, her Muslim novelty, her lapdog-like affection—in all, the extreme devotion of that thirteen-year-old girl unhinged me. Yvonne tried to get revenge on me by inviting Moreau to comfort her. But this enraged Flora, who shaved her head in reprisal. In retaliation, the man from Marseilles set Flora's curtains on fire and was caught trying to escape in Sousse. The Kairouan police never got him. And, you know, even Yvonne, deep down, had been hoping to see them put him away!

The brothel in Sousse was small. The room where they entertained the soldiers had started to fall apart along the base of the walls, which had started to crumble into the adjoining rooms. The doors to these other rooms could no longer open all the way. It was an exclusive sort of place, in its way. Not too many clients could be allowed in at once. The house was too small, but our patience was philosophical—which only increased the danger: it was a channeled, potent, prodigious force. Fifty, eighty, a hundred men shaking with desire, worn out from jealousy, from fear, and hungry for flesh, all stuck in the same place and waiting for the same thing—this turned us into a single terrible Cyclops that rumbled outside the single bedroom, shifting its weight listlessly. Eighty men perfumed with vinegar, nutmeg, pepper, and cloves, slowly conglomerating into one big slab of meat, one creature, threatening and blind.

You could hear it knocking its forehead against the walls. The chairs collapsed under its weight, and then the rumor of a longer wait—faint as oil, quick as acid—penetrated into the cracks, ran level with the walls, into the plaza. Sometimes it looked like a stream of water, other times a line of ants, and occasionally the black of barbed wire . . .

Have you heard the creaking of a transatlantic ship, surrounded by the ocean? That was the creaking of the walls of Esther the Jew's room when our little symposium happened to go on and on, and my pleasure monopolized her all through the night. Have you ever heard people talk about the shadows of the departed passing over the roofs of the houses where they died? Well, we saw the restless silhouettes of the satyrs waiting and waiting in the confines of the brothel. The nightmares that disturbed my sleep in Esther's room were unending. In my dreams, the troops of the Forty-Sixth Infantry would never forgive me. They couldn't help it. Their desire was hanging out of their flies, camped along the walls of Alexandria, banging on the walls of Esther's room until the walls felt as though they would collapse at last and suffocate me . . . But no, little by little desire realized the uselessness of its efforts and astutely took a different tack. It came up to the door but it couldn't slide open the shutter-bolt. It doesn't have hands, you see. It leaned on the door and pushed. The door was elastic. It seemed to give way only to become more rigid thereafter. From my bed, I watched this bloody struggle between cedar of Lebanon and stray desire—and admired the door's triumph in the end.

Already, the sun was coming in through the cracks of the poorly insulated room and the house eunuch was shaking out the rugs, which now seemed hardened with spit, like the thorny leaves of prickly pears.

Have I already mentioned that one of my relatives was myopic and an eye doctor and that he fished with a tall reed, looking through opera glasses? His near-sightedness imposed a necessary punctiliousness to his move-ments and even intentions. As a result, he was meticulous in all things. I inherited his enormous delight in neatness. Seeing is already a pleasure, but clarity makes it a pleasure twice over. Would that I could use microscope lenses as my spectacles. Winter always enticed me to the windows of my room, to watch the sad lives of our townspeople blanketed in snow, and so, in the months beforehand, I always made certain to prepare my observatory: I cleaned the windowpanes with such care that they seemed almost nonexistent in their translucency. Flies, still unaware of the invention of glass, tried to come in from the street, dying from the impact. I've watched them dying, in piles, writhing around uselessly, deliciously, trying in vain to prolong their existence. But winter slaughtered them nonetheless in the ambush of my clear glass. And I, behind this glass, watched them die.

After two years away, I found myself returning to Bougival with Raimundo the coachman today. He was much older. His hair had grayed dramatically. "The snow of the years"—such an affected, romantic image. Gray mold instead of hair. Not so much conquered by time as by the elements.

Should I have asked about his life? No. It's easy to read a single newspaper from start to finish, but an entire year's worth is more likely to make you want to run away . . . And that's the impression Raimundo gave. An enormous bundle of newspapers, too imposing to dip into, despite the interesting things one might learn . . .

"And how have you been?" he asked instead. Next to his life as a coachman-drifter, running to so many volumes, my own adventures would fill only a few measly sentences . . . "What do you bring us from Africa?"

"Syphilis," I replied mechanically.

Raimundo didn't seem the least bit surprised. Perhaps he would have found it far stranger had I returned with nothing at all. I was surprised at my honesty, but how could I consider hiding anything from this most supreme confessor—particularly the interior drama I was then experiencing, the impetus to the greatest art that one can dream of attaining: at once the lion and the Christian in the arena of the soul . . . ?

"And what are you going to do about it?" he asked me sarcastically—the old pachyderm.

"I'm thinking about writing a book," I said, "a book that would be a sort of symptomatic journal of my disease that could serve as a source of information for doctors and literary types both. This idea came knocking at my door as twilight fell . . . I let it seduce me as though I were just another conquest . . . Even though I know that writing a book is the greatest shame that an original mind can bring upon itself.

"But—I want to write a book, Raimundo. A book that will make my illness into an iridescent fantasy . . ."

"Then there's only one thing that can be holding you back," my coachman replied, "and it's worrying that women won't want you once they read about your life. But I don't think that'll happen in your case. Women love to love degenerates, you know. When you make it public that you're now what the better wives in town like to refer to oh so poetically as 'badly indisposed,' then, only then will you find out what it truly is to be loved! You'll acquire—oh, conquering hero!—the allure of the dangerous. Till now, the only way to make yourself seem so attractive was to make it known that you're a libertine with a trail of pregnant, brokenhearted victims in your wake! In future, however, that petty sort of allure will give way to a new form of voluptuousness—the syphilitic! It will be the fourth forbidden form of sensuality to add to your store. You've quite exhausted the other three: abortion, menstruation, and the douche . . .

"But I digress: a symptomatic journal, you say?"

"Yes, yes . . . already the disease snakes through me . . . the curling tendrils of love and syphilis—one of absolute purity, the other . . . how to describe it?"

"Call it the glory of Don Juan!" said Raimundo. "And, look, if you have the courage to give away your secrets in this book, don't hesitate to make Don Juan your protagonist! Imagine how beautiful it would be . . . the only thing that's missing from the story of Don Juan—who's really nothing more than an artificial phallus, a masturbatory fantasy for Catholic women—is his being syphilitic . . ."

"I'll consider it," I told him, and got down from the coachbox ready to write my first chapter.

You'll never know the true depths of the abyss without first probing the mouth of your own syphilitic chancre. The tiny excavation this silent worker etches into your trusting skin will show you the deep darkness of eternity. Being marked in this way, with a crater on one's body, a crater that can easily be covered with cotton, is a sign that one has been found worthy of the beauty bestowed by God, who paves some pathways with precious stones and renders others impassable . . . It's not my fault I've been given such an honor. My son's nasal septum, which syphilis will erode, will make him look like Socrates: a good subject for future statuary. (Hereditary syphilis, our own wise men say, affects the nasal septum.) That son of an Athenian midwife didn't leave any written works, after all—he's known only by his bust. See how the ages have esteemed him. His snub nose was unbreakable—the perfect nose to be sculpted in stone. It lends itself to solidity. What makes for ugliness in life ought to help make one eternal, no? Why bother filling up the libraries with works of genius? All those stone Socratic heads—with no sharp angles, and therefore no structural weaknesses—have stayed intact despite the centuries, despite the iconoclasts, despite rival philosophers. It was enough for Socrates to be syphilitic to be right.

Look, the type of Don Juan you should put in this book you're threatening us with—well, maybe you could base him on a particular exemplar of the type, whose confession I used to take, and who, today, in my capacity as coachman, I don't really mind exposing to public scrutiny . . .

"I'm not going to say he was the Don Juan known as the Comte de Lauzun, who supposedly slept with Louis XIV's sister—not at all. He was a tall man, with a majestic stride, brown hair, green eyes. There was no intrigue about him. Nobody would have said he was an exotic sort. His physique wasn't what you'd call impressive and his clothes weren't elegant. He was a man—simply a man—neither seductive nor disagreeable. He went home early every night to his bachelor quarters. His nights were long. He was past his prime. No longer chasing after women. But under his exterior calm, the old viper inside him hadn't grown old in the least. Like some sinister laboratory tucked away at the far end of a vacant lot, or hidden behind the shady trees at the back of a hospital, he was discreet and terrible, having taken refuge in his bachelor's quarters only to refine and concentrate his art.

"What could this Don Juan do in the silences of his life? Write and dream alone. He filled his time writing letters. First he would write out multiple drafts that he'd read aloud to himself and of course adore. Then he'd recopy these and pepper them with plenty of adjectives, employing the clumsy style of an unlettered amateur, but still full of all the requisite poetic imagery, since, he said, 'Women are birds you must hunt with metaphor.' This self-deluded magician even had the cleverness to seal his letters with a tear shed in the loneliness of his nights! All this effort no doubt was intended to increase the trivial charm of his epistles—in much the same way as an actor will make himself cry real tears on stage in order to convince you that you are watching an excellent performance.

"After finishing his latest missive, this old bachelor would open his window to listen to the beating heart of the night. Until this moment his bedroom had been hermetically sealed—he could only write when absolutely isolated at his desk. If outsiders could see him there, his love-missives would've been cheapened by this exposure . . . or he would have lost a little dignity, revealed in all his solitude . . . but, in any case . . . he died writing. Each of his letters was like *La Peau de chagrin*—baring his soul, his great spiritual devotion . . . His letters were a way of maintaining his persona, you see: he couldn't bear to see himself as a failure. He liked to say to women, 'You know, my dear, our souls are just so many little pieces of paper,' and he said this precisely because he hoped that, if anyone gathered up his correspondence, they would find his soul there intact . . . like the painted scene we reassemble through the reconstruction of an ancient Etruscan vase."

Did my father intend to make something of me? I don't know. I was seventeen and only went home to eat or sleep. I spent the rest of the day along the river or at our neighbors'. Not because I was much of a conversationalist, but it's nice on occasion to return to something resembling civilization.

Now and then someone died in the next town over, Croissic, where I went sometimes, more or less mechanically, crossing the bridge that leads away from the heart of Bougival. The town crier would announce the death, always trying to end on a cheerful note. Since his trade was an endangered one, the crier did everything he could to get the neighborhood's sympathy. Whenever he gathered a crowd, following his usual drum roll, the crier would turn to comedy . . .

The people who died were generally unknown to me. Women who'd spent their lives in the shadows of their own pantries, confining themselves to their rooms or beds in their final years. Raising my eyes toward the peculiar windows of many a small town, I've surprised plenty of these lifelong maidservants who never so much as take a little walk down the street to get some sun. Faded old women, the majority of them, who didn't bother with brushes or combs, keeping their hair in place with ribbons, as was the style in 1830. Some of them were skinny and faded but others had faces that had grown wide and snub-nosed from so much staring—like Sœur Anne, the sister of Bluebeard's last wife . . .

These women generally died between the ages of ninety and ninety-five. The official statistics from the mayor's office would prove me right. The thought of anyone living for so many years made me a little emotional. I never missed their funerals. I followed their processions as though walking behind an itinerant Peripatetic philosopher, reflecting on the fact that these women now on their way to their graves never experienced a day in their lives that was more intense or important than any other: the years had simply been a continual autumn for their souls, which shed one leaf at a time until they were bare—even the birthdays just another little loss. Those pitiful centenarians, who shriveled like oranges in their miserable skins, acquired something in death that moved me . . . the way the plaintive notes of a cathedral organ might move me as well.

Was it the satisfaction of knowing life wouldn't be sullied by these women any longer? Was it the sense that the earth was somehow taking a belated revenge upon them that made me happy? That the earth that was going to fold these already mysterious old ladies into its subterranean mystery? I don't know what it was, really. But suspecting that my own end wouldn't be too long in coming, those old women's deaths gave me just as much pleasure as the prospect of having to watch my brilliant youth waste away in some moth-eaten chest of drawers in the granaries of my gray village—pulverized by the great cumbersome bulk of time—made me absolutely miserable.

Their funerals truly moved me. These old women had exhausted life, drinking up even more air than the young. In their homes, bottled up along with their fortunes, rents, retirement money or state pension, they'd retained throughout their lives all the skittish self-interest of those people who never bother to put up a fight, but simply withdraw, preemptively, when there's any fear of losing ground—sealing themselves in their rooms as if in a fort. Above all, however, these women moved me because they'd been virgins for ninety years—far longer than Joan of Arc had suffered from that affliction. As long as the statues of Joan of Arc.

Generally, the trips that my friend the coachman took me on were from the stables to Mont Valérien. Happy as the dawn, my charioteer would depart for Paris, estimating his day's tips. But one winter night I found him along the road from Chatou to Rueil, along the Seine, his coach was tracing a series of *S*s like a staggering drunk. Not really wanting to, he accepted my company on the coachbox. He talked to himself. After some time, he decided to explain the cause of his uneasiness—his voice hoarse, croaking with rage, bombastic, as he affirmed the following (letting his reins fall in the process, always the sign of a coachman who's lost control):

"Look—when you hear that someone's snuck into a jeweler's through the sewers or the municipal water pipes and the walls have been drilled through and the tile floor's been ripped out, the perpetrator is almost certainly a hunchback.

"Did you know that by the fourth century, there was a distinct race of hunchbacks flourishing in the Byzantine Empire? Today this race is nearly extinct, though new, atavistic examples occasionally recur. The few specimens still alive come out only at night, under the arch of the railway bridge.

"When the signal lights go from red to green and, as happens from time to time, two trains collide on the tracks, it's not unusual for a hunchback in a nearby hovel to step out to entertain himself with the crunching of their vertebrae, the grand horrific spectacle of two mathematical axes meeting in a terrifying geometrical equation, their polygons making nonsense of the imaginary points once delineated by their locomotives, not to mention the impassive parallels of their tracks. It is the hunchback, you see, who's engineered these astounding and macabre orgies of destruction, walking happily through the carnage thereafter to gather up, where he may, those pulpy bits of brain that, in the ashes of the inferno, look like giant mushrooms that have sprouted from this new lake of blood, upon which float the dining car's silver serving trays, and from which, in places, one may see the silver handles of drowned sugar bowls reaching into the air. The hunchback amuses himself by fishing out the bowls while the surface of the pool of blood coagulates according to the same fatal law that produces a crust of salt at the edges of the Dead Sea . . .

"Rome and Greece exposed such hunchbacks at birth. Medieval kings tied them to the foot of their thrones with heavy chains so that their snarls would remind them of the snarling of the discontented peasantry. The hunchback is a sign of revolution against all things! The hunchback is failure made flesh, and his hate flourishes in inverse proportion to his smallness. His kind revolted the queens of old so much that when a lady from court became pregnant, they covered their royal hunchbacks with tar and started a bonfire for good luck. That's how they invented fireworks, you know . . ."

The coachman went quiet a moment. He seemed more at ease now, like an asthmatic finally able to breathe. He added: "A hunchback just mugged me back there on the corner and because of his size I didn't even see which way he went! He took off with nine francs . . ."

Catholic liturgy has conquered women. It's the same as with skylarks and mirrors. Anyone who adopts religion's deep and pompous tone can easily win a woman over. This is the reason I've always tried my best to be as affected and ceremonious as possible. And there's another reason too: I take my Latin roots quite seriously—I might speak French, but I count my lovers in Italian. Roots, I might add, with a Saracen sadness just beneath.

Syphilis is a civilized disease, and I intend to declare my allegiance to its aesthetic. I acquired it in the most charming of ways. Suffice to say, she who bestowed this gift upon me did so with the same ease and elegance as the doves of Aphrodite must alight upon the breasts of sleeping women . . .

My nights have always been fragmentary. I've never slept through the night. I have attacks that aren't quite insomnia. They're interruptions in the pleasant—literary—death that is sleep, though they are always kind enough to retie the loose ends of my unfinished nightmares when they depart.

These attacks have their origins in my childhood. In the Jesuit school where I was a student after my mother's death, a bell would ring at random times in the night, always well after twelve, obliging us to sit up in our beds and recite a creed. Afterward, we were meant to go back to sleep as though there had been no interruption.

This custom was something like torture for my classmates and myself, particularly at the beginning of the school year.

At last I yielded to the routine that has undone my nights ever since. What was the reason behind those bells, I wondered, always pealing at such an inconvenient hour?

Few Jesuits were able clear up this secret, but eventually one of the Reverend Fathers explained it to me:

When the honest Society of Jesus possessed its most prosperous missions in the Viceroyalty of the Río de la Plata, the Indians who fell under its guardianship—exhausted by their brutal, crushing workdays—took no pleasure in their marriage beds. Husbands simply slept beside their legal partners every night without fulfilling their conjugal obligations. Thus, in those lands—generally thought of as a fertile paradise—the locals quickly developed a birth-rate problem.

A priest came up with the idea of the late-night bell as a means of correcting this problem. Once the Indians had been reinvigorated by a few hours of rest—interrupted by the bell—and lay back down having recited their creed, they found their women waiting for them, and soon rediscovered their appetites.

And so the Jesuit bells continued ringing this strange peal for married couples—rung by celibates who'd taken vows of chastity and always went about with eyes cast down. These insomniacs are truly worthy of the lowest third of Dante's hell—if they don't manage to invent an even more terrible place for themselves.

I'm waiting for bad news. Everything that passes near seems to bring it. There it is in those footsteps, retreating along the hall of this hotel. Somebody lacking the courage to knock! The rug in the hallway, accomplice to cowards, ends just outside my door, so once-silent footsteps resound there all at once on the floorboards, revealing the presence of a messenger . . . Who is it? Is he tall and thin like a ghost covered in a sheet? Or maybe he's more rotund, since I can hear him brushing against the walls. He's crossed the hall now. Farther off, a child's crying. He's scared. Like me, he senses danger; he cries inconsolably. The unknown that lurks in the corridor is pressing down on the fontanel in his skull, which has yet to close, and he understands the ebb and flow of the unfinished brain beneath. This child is breathing the same atmosphere in which I'm suffocating. He has a feeling he shouldn't drink any more of his mother's milk. His navel is doing the nervous dance of a cork in water. He feels the knot in his intestines unraveling, as if his interior equilibrium is about to be lost entirely—as though his entire body, that receptacle, were overflowing. Wax is pouring from his ears, and behind the wax is the fifth humor, the quintessence, which is the celestial ether and the honor of families.

The boy falls silent. A great current of air passes through the hall. Has the intruder departed? Everything shakes. Microbes jump into the air and then meander like sleepwalkers at hand-height. Nobody collects them, so they return to the carpet.

The ogre has disappeared. He was scared off by the ringing of a bell, a murmuring, a walking grumble wearing an apron and two big shoes—the bellhop, who just walked down the hall.

How many kilometers have I traveled in pursuit of a woman's breast! I'd lose count before I reached a number. And only for a breast! The rest of the body is irrelevant.

The days seem sad to me, and the nights even more so, if I don't close my eyes and concentrate on the memory of breasts past. Loose breasts and barely glimpsed breasts, enormous breasts, breasts standing at attention. I've followed thousands of women. Two, three a day, interrupting my work, forgetting where I was headed, missing my train, crossing the road, tripping over rough ground, descending into empty basements, spying through keyholes—all for a glimpse of the secret gifts women carry with them. I've lived my life dreaming of a pyramid of various breasts—the way Tamerlane dreamed of pyramids of skulls.

I've asked myself on several occasions who lives in certain houses in Bougival. The houses with the blinds closed, the doors locked. There's never a servant out on the patio. Maybe one cat or another. Sometimes two or three pigeons climbing up a cornice, like neighbors come for a visit, using their beaks to tidy the great starched folds of their white skirts . . .

Men die centenarians without ever having known a woman. All they know is a braid, an eye, a buttock, a leg, or breast, as I have.

It's the fetish we acquire at fourteen, looking through the keyhole in a door, when masturbating like a person cleaning a nozzle simply for the pleasure of seeing it clean. Later, the body searches for relief, and later still, when a woman truly takes hold of us, it's enough just to remember a single one of her garments, her profile, perfume, presence, or smile . . .

Cities are places where love is quite civilized, so when a man finds himself face to face with such a woman, these two beings—who, without admitting it, both long for the satisfaction of their many acquired vices in the most ideal possible setting and circumstances—merely head home and masturbate. Once again, the man has the opportunity to possess this woman's leg, buttocks, neck, tongue, or breasts—her eyes deep and intense, or else blue and innocent. In this way, indeed, the same woman can serve for a hundred half-men. They don't get jealous. Each one has his part of her.

This isn't conjecture. Man even dies without knowing his own wife. What is it that he loves in her, if not what he loved in the opposite sex back when he was a full-time masturbator? He's still never experienced the love of an entire woman. Might the fault lie with the clothing that hides her entirety from us? It's society that only offers her up to us piecemeal and forces us to masturbate until our deaths . . . If women went about naked, the absence of mystery would make us purer-minded, and it would take quite an effort for us to single out or dwell upon one part of her body alone. Her entire body should give us an *aesthetic* rather than *voluptuous* pleasure. For now, however, our world remains stuck at the keyhole, where we saw her for the first time . . . We only see a leg, an arm, a breast.

Cotton mittens bother me when they're dyed black. They always give me a little shiver of disgust. It's the dead hand still alive underneath the dyed cotton. I can smell the winding sheets that hang on the walls during wakes and are usually damp and sometimes have silvery gray hairs still stuck in them . . .

Joy is in the light-colored glove one puts on in the morning, getting out of bed. Together with a striped sock.

We've entered a new world. Its geographic limits are unknown. But every moment that transpires within is torture. The round moon tonight is a server's tray sent up from hell. It's yellow in color, but it wants to be red, like the sputum of some tubercular titan . . .

The calves born tonight all have six legs and glassy eyes. They'll enter the alcoholic eternity of our museums in due time. Much as a villager's boy—a seventh son—will end up in the city with a number on his chest, in the lunatic asylum, in the prison, or in the hospital. And then, tonight, there is a villager who will hang himself in the malignant shadow of our fig tree; the moon makes him think long and hard during his last moments alive.

Water and foamy piss overflow from the urinals. Beyond the star-shaped holes in their drains—in the cotton wads of the diseased—things have gotten clogged: there is emptiness and desperation in our drainpipes.

The neighborhood roosters get restless too early and, as if passing over row after row of fences, a train whistle scratches the silence.

Danger prowls around the patio.

Its eyes stop on the latches and study the bolts.

Silence like an arid field.

Silence like a seeded field.

The childlike scream of the train rages in the ravine of midnight. It's left the rail yard. It surges on. Filled to the brim with the diseased.

Heading to the south, it leads little girls by their limp hands . . . those who had to interrupt their eternal dialogue on the subject of fashion while saying their good-byes on the platform—for fashion reigns even in a sanatorium. It carries diabetic mothers to Vichy. To Venice, Cairo or Bruges, it carries eighteenth-century lovers. The ones who still write love letters, I mean. It carries abbesses and seminarians, trading their convents and monasteries for moral turpitude. It carries bored people in search of the right bridge or lead cathedral roof from which to hurl themselves. Two of the train cars are full of tiny instructional skeletons from Paris classrooms that the municipality is sending to the seaside developments in Berck. Likewise, there's a mechanic on board who will lose his mind en route and sail past the last station without stopping. And in the boxcar harnessed to this magnificent realization of human progress is a corpse with no next of kin sent as priority cargo to arrive in Bordeaux before ten in the morning. It's his last appointment.

Such is the insomniac landscape that roasts me alive at night. It's that little girl who I kissed in the bushes on the tiny island north of Bougival who keeps me awake; I'm worried her parents are going to come looking for me. To keep myself busy while I wait, I've been shredding the tissue-paper fantasies of children between my fevered fingers—those same fantasies whose wings, deep in that little girl's soul, I managed to clip that afternoon . . . that girl on whom I left, for all time, my billy-goat fingerprints.

Could it be that the thing I'm missing is courage? That I simply lack the strength to a stab a stranger without fainting—risking my own life with such dangerous sport? If it seems easy, in theory, to kill, will it prove as easy to elude our consciences, which already begin to gnaw at us and betray us on the eve of our crime, even before the deed is done?

Courage is the literary vanity of criminals. Rarely is it hereditary, as for example in the Septeuil family.

I mean the famous young woman of the Septeuil line who drank a glass of human blood on the steps of the guillotine to save her father's, the Marquis', life. Now her descendants can stomach anything without fainting. They have the same ferocity in them. Her granddaughter, you know, already poor, unable to maintain the status the Restoration had granted her—a *duchesse brisée*, so to speak—and preferring to see the family horizontal than sitting in the wrong place, had the courage to take her young daughter, fourteen years old, to a brothel. She did her mother proud. During the Second French Empire, before going to work in the luxury brothels where she eloquently badmouthed Victor Hugo, she used to rush her clients in the brothel run by a second-rate madam, where she wore bright red satin slippers. An uncle of hers—her mother's brother, thus likewise of the Septeuil family line—soon found out his family name was being used as a doormat by city lowlifes and wealthy merchants both, and so had the courage, at seventy, to marry his niece, snatching her away to the best brothels in town, the very Stations of the Cross of sexual pleasure, at which he worshiped with the delight of a devotee, finally installing her in one of Paris's most celebrated basilicas of love.

I 've always searched for the love I didn't possess. I tried to be loved. I did everything I could. That's all I ever did. Builders risk falling like bricks from their scaffolding. They lose arms and legs. I've never lost anything, and yet I've lost everything. Just to be wanted.

There's nothing more in life than to love someone. To be loved. Such is the happy monotony of my life.

NOVEMBER 1, 18 —

I don't know whether to stay or go. Nothing frightens me more than the prospect of failing to live up to the great spiritual responsibility my mother laid upon me. She thought I was a man who would never know failure. She expected so much of me, I worry I'll leave my job unfinished.

I am her optimism. I am the player through whom she sought to wreak vengeance on this world in which men forced her to live—because, like all our perfect Spanish mothers, there was no treasure for her in this life, no jewelry to adorn her, save the leaden melancholy that came upon her as her dreams flowed away, like water over river stones in the afternoon.

If I wrote a book about Don Juan's syphilis, I'd worry about acquiring that habit or weakness of writers who plot out all their actions as though for a book, writers whose days have become the monotonous pages of a novel. A book is a secret vice. If we could collect all our dandruff as easily as we collect the so-called contents of our heads, it would be just as publishable. Like the eighteenth-century woman who liked lace so much she cut it up and ate it in a tortilla, there are people who worship the fetish object that is a book and want nothing more than to see themselves reflected in it—like Narcissus.

I'd also like to avoid the mania of writing books to serve as funeral wreaths. I remember some grief-stricken parents who published a book about a daughter of theirs who'd died at the age of eighteen. Now, what could that poor anonymous girl have accomplished at such a young age to warrant such a tribute? Two photographs included in the text gave us the measure of this extinct creature. In one of them the girl is playing croquet. She'd played just once, in a hotel I used to frequent. Hardly a devotee!

The other photograph showed her on a horse. A few minutes after the picture was taken, the horse bucked the girl off and she broke her leg.

The seeming pedigree of such images made her parents forget the facts. Writers are the same.

They publish books for the pleasure of seeing them printed and bound, without remembering that the saddest aspects of their lives will end up contained in those pages.

But wouldn't my book be the result of my desire to commit a crime, and thus be a part of it? Wouldn't every page be a sliver of glass in the daily soup of my fellow citizens?

A book is the vegetal pulp left behind by man. And now, after countless centuries of digging up and studying palimpsests and engraved tablets, they're saying that we should just allow all those dead, abandoned cities to become buried again beneath the windblown sediment . . .

A book is a slow, unavoidable catastrophe.

I've put my box of calomel aside and now sit, thinking. My eyes wander from the page of the daybook that the wind's finger has just turned and from there to the valise sitting in the corner like it just got back from a trip. On a loose page, I've written: "The days go on . . . literature and fame both distress me. Neither of them deserves my faith. It's been a long time since I've dreamed of an absolute repose. Death, perhaps. Art has poisoned existence. I'm discouraged. Trying to step beyond the commonplace, all I've accomplished is the loss of one of my legs. I should hate literature, feel disgust for it—no matter that it did me the meager favor of growing my wings . . ."

I could always forgive my mother having so many lovers singing her praises, but I have no patience for those harlots who spend their lives letting men talk them into sucking their marrow out, so to speak. And then, worse still, there are certain corrupt women who elevate this activity by putting molasses on their lover's equipment, so as to make the experience sweeter. But even these women, beneath contempt, cannot compete with some of the more impressive sorts of degenerate—like, for instance, literature. Literature does far worse things than those poor whores who, out of hunger, have to turn tricks from street corner to street corner on the outskirts of town. Literature is invited into the family home as easily as a maid—but soon is giving one breast to the son and the other to the father, kissing all the daughters with Sappho's lips, and disheartening the mother by giving her *The Little Flowers of St. Francis* to read. Me she nursed and later delivered to glory. She was far worse than a whore—she didn't even wash my private parts. Now I smell her perfume on every road. I've deposited all my assets into her account. I'm nothing when I'm far from her. What would I do if I couldn't set eyes on her from time to time? My mouth is full of consonants. Why don't I write verse? Because the grief of a poet is even greater than his work, and more worthy of praise. I write simply, never aiming for the stars.

No, no verse! No music! Let us be just as we are: unfinished things without rhythm. Time has gnawed away our hope, and while the dampness inside us ate away at our hearts and livers, literary types entertained us by painting false exits . . . Others collected human vulgarities and sold them in pill-form . . . And others still assembled catalogs of souls and wrote informative introductions to accompany them. Nobody has ever honestly shown us, for instance, a man precisely as he was during his transition from the countryside to the city. Authors have merely "discovered" psychology and thus complicated our knowledge of life even further. A psychologist doesn't understand people: he's a businessman who sells carnival costumes. There are no costumes, however, for the soul. No, there's nothing more there than its poor twisted simplicity, turned inside-out by a civilization still terrified of tigers—and hiding from them in cities.

There will come a day when no more poets will be born. The city, in our fearsome urbanized future, will impede their birth. And so, the government will keep the ones still made ill "by beauty and by the past" in gardens, like greenhouses, on the rooftops of skyscrapers, without demanding anything of them—much the way we now provide for the insane—leaving these geniuses free in their cages believing the lie that they might yet prettify the landscape of the apocalypse with their brilliance.

Raimundo wrinkled the space between his brows and said: "I've wanted to write a book many times. It's just that I've restrained myself. Since you're so determined to 'commit' this crime without delay, why don't you take advantage of this Don Juan story I'd have written in your place? So: Imagine that our Don Juan has a bigger supper than usual. He strokes a magnificent apricot in his palm for minutes at a time. The fruit's aroma makes the old room smell like springtime.

"When at last he peels the fruit, he does so on a plate that doesn't belong to his regular set of dishes. It slipped in among his regular china amid the forced intimacy experienced by delicate crockery and the clay pots all washed in the same kitchen sink. This piece is rose-colored porcelain, and one can read, in gold along its edge, the word 'Memento.'

"Later Don Juan goes out to the street, a Sunday in a Catholic city. The women have separated from the men; the men have gathered in groups to watch the city girls strolling by in pairs. The conventions of this puritanical city make the women appear distant and discolored to Don Juan—the way landscapes look through the tiny window of a stagecoach: landscapes of second-hand clothes shops, old abandoned stage sets, the gray halls at the Opera House ball on Ash Wednesday . . .

"Among the passersby, our Don spots a young man of about sixteen. An ephebe embodying all the ideal lines and curves of the classical concept of beauty, synthesized in the angels of *quattrocento painters*. An ephebe who's adopted a certain posture and yet seems possessed of a fragility—neither quality much in tune with this era. An ephebe who already feels— though still growing out the lower branches of his life—a desire for total revolution, real experience—the need to take hold of everything exceptional, a tendency toward a certain *me déshabiller de la vie*, as the poets say. Well, this ephebe now seems in a precarious sort of position, with Don Juan bearing down on him . . .

"Our Don feels an unknown pleasure seeing the beauty of this emissary. He follows the young man, straightening his tie as he goes, and starts a conversation with him. The ephebe does perceive his interlocutor, but does not react. Don Juan feels love, perhaps, for this lovely specimen of androgyny, who reminds him of an excessively beautiful woman, albeit without the same sense of being a living coat rack, which often distinguishes men from women . . . That is, a woman would have been better dressed.

"They get in a coach. As a coachman, I can't conceive of a novel without a coach ride in it. Don Juan points out the starry night sky to the young man, speaking of its hypothetical cartography as though it were nothing more than another city neighborhood, not a distant, magnificent thing. The young man, feeling merely decorative inside the coach, responds by moving the slanted almonds of his eyes. His lips are two pale roses.

"Now: Will Don Juan be able to refrain from ravishing this creature, who was born with a set of wings fit to take him to the very heights of passion—like all those who have been created expressly for love? He isn't just another woman, after all. He isn't even a decisive departure from womankind. He is the white marble statue who won the heart of the black king in the Louvre . . . The personification of the belated, literary decline of mystic love. Don Juan, after so many years—since his school days, in fact—submits then, in his coach, to the satisfactions of solitary pleasure.

"A sharp pain in his temples pierces his head as the shudder of pleasure subsides between the flaccid muscles of his thighs. He is tormented now by the specter of a humiliating death. And he says to his silent spectator:

"'Get out. I think I'm going to die. You would compromise my death.'

"But the ephebe responds, 'No—give me that most voluptuous pleasure for which I've been searching so long. What I've always wanted is to watch someone die . . .'

"Don Juan doesn't have the strength to object or prolong his conversation with this slender ambassador of carnality . . . and so dies a magnificent, sumptuous death with an angel at his side— just like the Bishop of Orléans, whose death you've already heard all about . . ."

When winter arrived, the Seine rose toward the sky, and clouds enveloped the village of Bougival along with the changing light at dawn and dusk. You could feel the cold of the water on your skin. The lighthouses, with their distant oil lamps, languished in a tangle of tulle.

On one of these nights, as the shimmer of one such light struggled to pierce the gloom, the silhouette of a man cut through the fog on one of the outlying streets of this uninteresting village. The light hit his face, and as soon as he stepped out of this luminous zone, he spotted me and stopped, startled. My path was decisive. I moved without hesitation. And my grim determination must have shocked this anxious passerby. I read the terror in his face. A wordless dread. His throat had gone dry. I looked him over: a poor devil, a wretch, somebody I could have killed without the least caution. He was already half dead. No cry for help would have tarnished his lips; there would be no struggle to impede my crime.

We lost each other again in the mist. My victim, perhaps, fell to the ground, faint with terror. I continued my march. There wasn't even a whisper. The winter mist had enveloped the world in its gray velvet.

I felt very alone. I began talking to myself in a loud voice and confessed the strange desire that this pale, trembling man had just woken in me. A man so frightened, at night, on an empty street . . . wouldn't he have been easy to finish off? I don't mean that I would have killed him right there, necessarily, where the green leaves of the hedge look as though they could have been painted in watercolors right on top of the fog, but perhaps further on, where his blood could have been mistaken for mud, where twelve hours would have to pass before the sun was bright enough to distinguish a corpse from a lump of refuse.

APRIL 4, 18—

I've sketched out my plans and am ready. I have a new strength in me, taken from the secret core of my life, driving me on, controlling me. It's health, youth, and optimism combined. Until yesterday, my tentative novel ("The Syphilis of Don Juan") served as a haven for my imagination. Today, it doesn't satisfy my thirst—or, better said, can no longer stem the anguish that gnaws at me on the eve of an act that is now quite inevitable. I'm halfway between a comedy and a strange sort of drama, and feel an overbearing need to lower the curtain. No simple curtain: the front curtain of the stage, the grand drape, the great iron and asbestos curtain that drops like a zinc plate from the sixth floor and creaks as it falls. Something like that, flamboyant, coarse, unexpected—something that will impose its tyranny over my life without question. I'm going to kill someone.

I'm not frightened, I'm not scared, I won't regret it.
I've resolved in advance all the premises I need to consider.

I've chosen my victim. Crossing the market, I passed a woman with blonde hair: thin, with sallow skin and washed-out blue eyes. I've seen her before aboard a Belgium-registered barge that was tied up at the end of the railway bridge.

The English are naturally aristocratic, so there's nothing more miserable than seeing one fallen on hard times. The need visible in their faces—shining through the miscellaneous grit covering their Apollonian features—pains me. My victim, with her delicate face, has forgotten that she's a woman and not some floozy. Boat grease clings to her tattered dress. She doesn't brush her hair anymore, just makes a knot of it at the nape of her neck. Her bodice is fastened with a safety pin—the button's fallen off. Clearly she isn't especially happy. If she doesn't drink in backroom bars, she certainly gives the impression of being an alcoholic; husbandless, discontent, feeling a general hostility toward the world.

As I passed her in the market, I found her concentrating heavily on some change she'd been thrown. She counted it coin by coin, like a child or a savage. Her slowness in counting, her obvious limited ability, made up my mind. It authorized my act. To unburden humanity of an imperfect being: a weakness.

He was born a Jew and into a career as an eye doctor. His clients went increasingly blind as he grew to adulthood with the grandfather who'd built their house. His grandfather died, and soon Alfredo Chascock invented a solution he claimed was the best remedy for any eye disease. He wouldn't sell it or give it away. His clients had to let him drip it over their infected eyes at the highest temperature they could bear. This portentous eyewash was simply water.

Alfredo Chascock had no other hobbies besides fishing, but his naturally dishonest nature had poeticized this activity. He bought salt-water fish from the market and showed them off as if he'd caught them in the river. Chascock was, as I've mentioned, myopic. Along with his fishing rod, he brought some opera glasses to better observe the lush, sinuous line of the Seine.

When I arrived that afternoon under the railway bridge, I saw Alfredo Chascock in a gully along the bank on the other side. He blended in with the tree trunk he was perched on. My eyes took in every detail, however, and couldn't help registering his presence there. The iron bridge seemed like a frame put around the sky: it was that immense and high.

In that valley, a natural avenue through the world, a gray-green landscape the color of grapes, the only dark spot was a barge tied up with various cables to the posts along the bank.

The barge was empty and without ballast. It bobbed up out of the water like a loose buoy. There were stairs that ran from the riverbank up to the deck where various geranium pots, lined up along the edge, brought to mind the cornices of the houses in Seville.

The scene was calm and mute. The waters of the Seine unraveled effortlessly, rolling forth like a ball of yarn. Every once in a while, a bang came from the barge, the sound multiplied in its empty holds. It was the blonde. I watched for two hours as she came and went from the top of the barge. She was making dinner. A tuft of blue smoke rose from a corrugated iron pipe and moved toward the middle of the river where swallows were flying—the low smoke the only indication that time was passing.

Chascock put the tilapia he'd just taken from the water into his buckets. I was alone. There were no witnesses and I started up the stairs.

I felt something in my heart. A thread broken away from its puppet. I looked back toward the bridge and was amazed. There was a person standing in precisely the same spot where I'd been observing my victim and awaiting the right moment to act. There was no doubt he was looking directly at me. Had he followed me here? I made a terrible grimace at him. I don't think he could've seen it from so far away, but my intentions undoubtedly came across, since the man, who knows why, left his vantage point and disappeared. Once again I was alone. I stepped up onto the barge's deck. It was cold on the tarred surface.

What was my victim doing? I crouched and looked into the hold that served as her room. She was peeling potatoes, prolifically, slowly. I treaded lightly and slid through the aft hatch. I started down the stairs. The boat tilted sternward. I wanted to reach the woman without being heard and sink my dagger into the nape of her neck the way it's done with calves at the butcher's. Every millimeter of this abrupt thrust would be felt in my hand. Her skin, cartilage, bones, maybe even her marrow all offering that delicious resistance which is the assassin's ultimate pleasure. Marrow? Would it be easy to cut through to it? And I thought of Neolithic caves full of horse bones, our delighted ancestors sucking out the fresh marrow, their spoils still warm, at least according to the deductions of certain paleontologists . . .

I was two steps from the blonde when she leaned down from her seat as if to pick up my shadow now extending over the basket she was reaching into for her potatoes. This woman who'd needed to count up her change so methodically in the market, and had done so with all the innocence of a lamb before an elegant wolf, had now assumed precisely the position I'd imagined for her, and I saw my hand reach for her, independent of my will, the gesture too swift for me to enjoy the knife's passage through her flesh.

I felt my hand tangled in her damp hair and the next instant a gush of blood surged against it and the edge of my knife.

That was when I let everything go, dropped the weapon and the woman I'd been holding up with the steel depths of my thrust. Her form crumpled, sagging into the potato basket, leaving one hand on the chair where she'd been sitting. Her other arm lay limp under the stove.

I blinked. I wanted to see something more, to feel something new, but that was all there was. I heard a buzzing in my ears, and there was a veil over my eyes. I was a nobleman "bescreen'd in night," as Shakespeare says. As I left, various chairs and a box got in my way. With great care, I managed to avoid them. I turned to study the scene and saw my victim had taken her hand off the chair and let it fall on the floor.

I lost my footing on the first step twice, and when my head poked back out over the hatch, there was a hiss like a snake's.

The fellow from a moment before was now up on the railway bridge looking down at the barge. He saw me, and just as I was about to tumble, weak-kneed, back down the stairs, he withdrew from the railing, equally terrified. I felt I'd been saved. I left the barge and climbed up the river bank.

From the lip of the valley, I looked back to commit it all to memory—the place where I'd just hurled myself into hell. On one side, the bridge closed the horizon. Beyond it, the hills above Marly and Mont Valérien. The Seine, like a great mirror, and the dark barge in the middle of the clear river. A bird and a dog passed nearby. The rippling of the water, before and after the barge. From time to time, a dull thud from the drumhead of my heart.

A group of men appeared on the opposite shore. I hid behind the lime trees. I followed them to the railway bridge. Rolling on the parapet, without falling into the water, was a cigarette butt. Someone had just left . . .

My eyes searched the crime scene. The barge jutted in and out of its waterline, the river toying with it. Nobody went near it. The damp path along the Seine ended there, where the water began. An hour passed. The sun went on its way. Alfredo Chascock parted the curtain of the horizon. I trembled.

Some timid fellow then appeared at the foot of the barge. It was the same one I'd seen on top of the bridge. He seemed to be imitating me. Did he think the barge was deserted? I hid to watch him more closely. He climbed onto the barge, walked across deck. Did he feel a shiver moving over the tar? At last he stopped and climbed down.

Alfredo Chascock was coming along the path near the barge. A man and a woman were following him.

A scream from inside the barge. The vessel heaved in the water as if there was a fight going on inside. The fellow from the bridge appeared again on deck. When they saw him, the man and the girl walking behind Alfredo Chascock started to walk faster. And then run. Alfredo Chascock must have heard some strange comment as they passed him. He perched his opera glasses on his nose.

But the man and the girl were now screaming too. The stranger on the barge ran from one end to the other. He didn't know what path to take. The open cuffs of his shirt, his hands, were both covered with blood. At last he scrambled down and ran off, and the man arriving with the girl took off after him. Both disappeared. The girl looked this way and that, sobbing hysterically without knowing why. Alfredo Chascock came over and tried to console her. The girl trusted in his soothing voice, which brought out from the depths of his throat the Jewish resignation engendered by so many centuries of massacres, and as if his words weren't enough, he gave her his opera glasses as well, so the girl could look up through them toward the bridge.

I could say that, physically, I was a happy man, as the night passed swiftly, profoundly, in my quiet bedroom, the clock on the nearby asylum marking the hours. I knew its chimes well, but had never felt the need to actually look out at the clock, which I imagined to be blind, without numerals.

At midnight yesterday, however, I passed in front of it. The clock let loose its chimes over sleepy Bougival and I lifted my eyes for the first time to the bell tower.

The clock wasn't a blind thing, an indifferent machine. No— connected to all the pain and misery here, the face of it was the yellowish face of a sickly moon, not an opaque pane covered with cabbalistic symbols.

How could it be that this same clock had marked my exis- tence until last night and made me hear what I believed were notes of jubilation? Had its face really been so dismal since the first night it was illuminated by an oil lamp, giving it the aspect of a dying star?

Can it be that I've only ever felt truly understood when the dismal notes of this sick clock consoled my heart? Has everything in me always breathed in reverse? Am I really so different from my fellow men?

p. 21   *Montaigne*: though it differs in places from Lascano Tegui's Spanish, we have used the Charles Cotton translation of the appropriate passage.

p. 103   *Greemvaneco*: probable Teguian distortion of "Van Eyck."

p. 135   *lowest third of Dante's hell*: in the Spanish, the narrator appears to be consigning these sadistic Jesuits to the third *circle* of hell. As Dante reserved this real estate for gluttons, we have taken a more liberal interpretation.

p. 138   *September*: this entry appears to be out of order, but we have elected to respect the sequence found in the original edition.

pp. 146–7   *Septeuil*: the apocryphal French Revolution story about a noblewoman forced by the mob to drink a glass of blood to save her father from execution in fact concerns the Marquis and Mademoiselle de Sombreuil, not Septeuil. The daughter died childless, years after the supposed incident.

p. 168   *bescreen'd in night*: *Romeo and Juliet*, Act 2, Scene 2. Translated literally, Tegui has his "nobleman" here "wrapped in a cloud."

EMILIO LASCANO TEGUI (1887–1966), a self-styled Viscount, is one of the most provocative and singular figures in Argentinian literature, making his way through life as a writer, journalist, curator, painter, decorator, diplomat, mechanic, gentleman, orator (known to make incendiary speeches in perfect rhymed verse), and even a dentist. His position as a translator for the International Post Office brought him to Europe, where he began his literary career.

IDRA NOVEY is a poet and translator. Her work has appeared in *Paris Review*, *Slate*, and the *Believer* and her debut collection *The Next Country* was released in 2008. She's received fellowships from the National Endowment for the Arts, the Poetry Society of America, and the PEN Translation Fund. She currently directs the Center for Literary Translation at Columbia University and teaches at Columbia and NYU.

PETROS ABATZOGLOU, *What Does Mrs. Freeman Want?*
MICHAL AJVAZ, *The Golden Age.*
The Other City.
PIERRE ALBERT-BIROT, *Grabinoulor.*
YUZ ALESHKOVSKY, *Kangaroo.*
FELIPE ALFAU, *Chromos.*
Locos.
IVAN ÂNGELO, *The Celebration.*
The Tower of Glass.
DAVID ANTIN, *Talking.*
ANTÓNIO LOBO ANTUNES, *Knowledge of Hell.*
ALAIN ARIAS-MISSON, *Theatre of Incest.*
IFTIKHAR ARIF AND WAQAS KHWAJA, EDS., *Modern Poetry of Pakistan.*
JOHN ASHBERY AND JAMES SCHUYLER, *A Nest of Ninnies.*
HEIMRAD BÄCKER, *transcript.*
DJUNA BARNES, *Ladies Almanack.*
Ryder.
JOHN BARTH, *LETTERS.*
Sabbatical.
DONALD BARTHELME, *The King.*
Paradise.
SVETISLAV BASARA, *Chinese Letter.*
RENÉ BELLETTO, *Dying.*
MARK BINELLI, *Sacco and Vanzetti Must Die!*
ANDREI BITOV, *Pushkin House.*
ANDREJ BLATNIK, *You Do Understand.*
LOUIS PAUL BOON, *Chapel Road.*
My Little War.
Summer in Termuren.
ROGER BOYLAN, *Killoyle.*
IGNÁCIO DE LOYOLA BRANDÃO, *Anonymous Celebrity.*
The Good-Bye Angel.
Teeth under the Sun.
Zero.
BONNIE BREMSER, *Troia: Mexican Memoirs.*
CHRISTINE BROOKE-ROSE, *Amalgamemnon.*
BRIGID BROPHY, *In Transit.*
MEREDITH BROSNAN, *Mr. Dynamite.*
GERALD L. BRUNS, *Modern Poetry and the Idea of Language.*
EVGENY BUNIMOVICH AND J. KATES, EDS., *Contemporary Russian Poetry: An Anthology.*
GABRIELLE BURTON, *Heartbreak Hotel.*
MICHEL BUTOR, *Degrees.*
Mobile.
Portrait of the Artist as a Young Ape.
G. CABRERA INFANTE, *Infante's Inferno.*
Three Trapped Tigers.
JULIETA CAMPOS, *The Fear of Losing Eurydice.*
ANNE CARSON, *Eros the Bittersweet.*
ORLY CASTEL-BLOOM, *Dolly City.*
CAMILO JOSÉ CELA, *Christ versus Arizona.*
The Family of Pascual Duarte.
The Hive.
LOUIS-FERDINAND CÉLINE, *Castle to Castle.*
Conversations with Professor Y.
London Bridge.

Normance.
North.
Rigadoon.
HUGO CHARTERIS, *The Tide Is Right.*
JEROME CHARYN, *The Tar Baby.*
MARC CHOLODENKO, *Mordechai Schamz.*
JOSHUA COHEN, *Witz.*
EMILY HOLMES COLEMAN, *The Shutter of Snow.*
ROBERT COOVER, *A Night at the Movies.*
STANLEY CRAWFORD, *Log of the S.S. The Mrs Unguentine.*
Some Instructions to My Wife.
ROBERT CREELEY, *Collected Prose.*
RENÉ CREVEL, *Putting My Foot in It.*
RALPH CUSACK, *Cadenza.*
SUSAN DAITCH, *L.C.*
Storytown.
NICHOLAS DELBANCO, *The Count of Concord.*
NIGEL DENNIS, *Cards of Identity.*
PETER DIMOCK, *A Short Rhetoric for Leaving the Family.*
ARIEL DORFMAN, *Konfidenz.*
COLEMAN DOWELL, *The Houses of Children.*
Island People.
Too Much Flesh and Jabez.
ARKADII DRAGOMOSHCHENKO, *Dust.*
RIKKI DUCORNET, *The Complete Butcher's Tales.*
The Fountains of Neptune.
The Jade Cabinet.
The One Marvelous Thing.
Phosphor in Dreamland.
The Stain.
The Word "Desire."
WILLIAM EASTLAKE, *The Bamboo Bed.*
Castle Keep.
Lyric of the Circle Heart.
JEAN ECHENOZ, *Chopin's Move.*
STANLEY ELKIN, *A Bad Man.*
Boswell: A Modern Comedy.
Criers and Kibitzers, Kibitzers and Criers.
The Dick Gibson Show.
The Franchiser.
George Mills.
The Living End.
The MacGuffin.
The Magic Kingdom.
Mrs. Ted Bliss.
The Rabbi of Lud.
Van Gogh's Room at Arles.
ANNIE ERNAUX, *Cleaned Out.*
LAUREN FAIRBANKS, *Muzzle Thyself.*
Sister Carrie.
LESLIE A. FIEDLER, *Love and Death in the American Novel.*
JUAN FILLOY, *Op Oloop.*
GUSTAVE FLAUBERT, *Bouvard and Pécuchet.*
KASS FLEISHER, *Talking out of School.*
FORD MADOX FORD, *The March of Literature.*
JON FOSSE, *Aliss at the Fire.*
Melancholy.

My Life in CIA.
Singular Pleasures.
The Sinking of the Odradek Stadium.
Tlooth.
20 Lines a Day.
JOSEPH MCELROY,
Night Soul and Other Stories.
ROBERT L. MCLAUGHLIN, ED.,
Innovations: An Anthology of Modern & Contemporary Fiction.
HERMAN MELVILLE, *The Confidence-Man.*
AMANDA MICHALOPOULOU, *I'd Like.*
STEVEN MILLHAUSER,
The Barnum Museum.
In the Penny Arcade.
RALPH J. MILLS, JR.,
Essays on Poetry.
MOMUS, *The Book of Jokes.*
CHRISTINE MONTALBETTI, *Western.*
OLIVE MOORE, *Spleen.*
NICHOLAS MOSLEY, *Accident.*
Assassins.
Catastrophe Practice.
Children of Darkness and Light.
Experience and Religion.
God's Hazard.
The Hesperides Tree.
Hopeful Monsters.
Imago Bird.
Impossible Object.
Inventing God.
Judith.
Look at the Dark.
Natalie Natalia.
Paradoxes of Peace.
Serpent.
Time at War.
The Uses of Slime Mould: Essays of Four Decades.
WARREN MOTTE,
Fables of the Novel: French Fiction since 1990.
Fiction Now: The French Novel in the 21st Century.
Oulipo: A Primer of Potential Literature.
YVES NAVARRE, *Our Share of Time.*
Sweet Tooth.
DOROTHY NELSON, *In Night's City.*
Tar and Feathers.
ESHKOL NEVO, *Homesick.*
WILFRIDO D. NOLLEDO,
But for the Lovers.
FLANN O'BRIEN,
At Swim-Two-Birds.
At War.
The Best of Myles.
The Dalkey Archive.
Further Cuttings.
The Hard Life.
The Poor Mouth.
The Third Policeman.
CLAUDE OLLIER, *The Mise-en-Scène.*
PATRIK OUŘEDNÍK, *Europeana.*
BORIS PAHOR, *Necropolis.*

FERNANDO DEL PASO,
News from the Empire.
Palinuro of Mexico.
ROBERT PINGET, *The Inquisitory.*
Mahu or The Material.
Trio.
MANUEL PUIG,
Betrayed by Rita Hayworth.
The Buenos Aires Affair.
Heartbreak Tango.
RAYMOND QUENEAU, *The Last Days.*
Odile.
Pierrot Mon Ami.
Saint Glinglin.
ANN QUIN, *Berg.*
Passages.
Three.
Tripticks.
ISHMAEL REED,
The Free-Lance Pallbearers.
The Last Days of Louisiana Red.
Ishmael Reed: The Plays.
Reckless Eyeballing.
The Terrible Threes.
The Terrible Twos.
Yellow Back Radio Broke-Down.
JEAN RICARDOU, *Place Names.*
RAINER MARIA RILKE, *The Notebooks of Malte Laurids Brigge.*
JULIÁN RÍOS, *The House of Ulysses.*
Larva: A Midsummer Night's Babel.
Poundemonium.
AUGUSTO ROA BASTOS, *I the Supreme.*
DANIËL ROBBERECHTS,
Arriving in Avignon.
OLIVIER ROLIN, *Hotel Crystal.*
ALIX CLEO ROUBAUD, *Alix's Journal.*
JACQUES ROUBAUD, *The Form of a City Changes Faster, Alas, Than the Human Heart.*
The Great Fire of London.
Hortense in Exile.
Hortense Is Abducted.
The Loop.
The Plurality of Worlds of Lewis.
The Princess Hoppy.
Some Thing Black.
LEON S. ROUDIEZ,
French Fiction Revisited.
VEDRANA RUDAN, *Night.*
STIG SÆTERBAKKEN, *Siamese.*
LYDIE SALVAYRE, *The Company of Ghosts.*
Everyday Life.
The Lecture.
Portrait of the Writer as a Domesticated Animal.
The Power of Flies.
LUIS RAFAEL SÁNCHEZ,
Macho Camacho's Beat.
SEVERO SARDUY, *Cobra & Maitreya.*
NATHALIE SARRAUTE,
Do You Hear Them?
Martereau.
The Planetarium.
ARNO SCHMIDT, *Collected Stories.*
Nobodaddy's Children.

SELECTED DALKEY ARCHIVE PAPERBACKS

CHRISTINE SCHUTT, *Nightwork.*
GAIL SCOTT, *My Paris.*
DAMION SEARLS, *What We Were Doing and Where We Were Going.*
JUNE AKERS SEESE,
  Is This What Other Women Feel Too?
  What Waiting Really Means.
BERNARD SHARE, *Inish.*
  Transit.
AURELIE SHEEHAN,
  Jack Kerouac Is Pregnant.
VIKTOR SHKLOVSKY, *Knight's Move.*
  A Sentimental Journey: Memoirs 1917–1922.
  Energy of Delusion: A Book on Plot.
  Literature and Cinematography.
  Theory of Prose.
  Third Factory.
  Zoo, or Letters Not about Love.
CLAUDE SIMON, *The Invitation.*
PIERRE SINIAC, *The Collaborators.*
JOSEF ŠKVORECKÝ, *The Engineer of Human Souls.*
GILBERT SORRENTINO,
  Aberration of Starlight.
  Blue Pastoral.
  Crystal Vision.
  Imaginative Qualities of Actual Things.
  Mulligan Stew.
  Pack of Lies.
  Red the Fiend.
  The Sky Changes.
  Something Said.
  Splendide-Hôtel.
  Steelwork.
  Under the Shadow.
W. M. SPACKMAN,
  The Complete Fiction.
ANDRZEJ STASIUK, *Fado.*
GERTRUDE STEIN,
  Lucy Church Amiably.
  The Making of Americans.
  A Novel of Thank You.
LARS SVENDSEN, *A Philosophy of Evil.*
PIOTR SZEWC, *Annihilation.*
GONÇALO M. TAVARES, *Jerusalem.*
LUCIAN DAN TEODOROVICI,
  Our Circus Presents . . .
STEFAN THEMERSON, *Hobson's Island.*
  The Mystery of the Sardine.
  Tom Harris.
JOHN TOOMEY, *Sleepwalker.*
JEAN-PHILIPPE TOUSSAINT,
  The Bathroom.
  Camera.
  Monsieur.
  Running Away.
  Self-Portrait Abroad.
  Television.
DUMITRU TSEPENEAG,
  Hotel Europa.
  The Necessary Marriage.
  Pigeon Post.
  Vain Art of the Fugue.
ESTHER TUSQUETS, *Stranded.*

DUBRAVKA UGRESIC,
  Lend Me Your Character.
  Thank You for Not Reading.
MATI UNT, *Brecht at Night.*
  Diary of a Blood Donor.
  Things in the Night.
ÁLVARO URIBE AND OLIVIA SEARS, EDS.,
  Best of Contemporary Mexican Fiction.
ELOY URROZ, *Friction.*
  The Obstacles.
LUISA VALENZUELA, *He Who Searches.*
MARJA-LIISA VARTIO,
  The Parson's Widow.
PAUL VERHAEGHEN, *Omega Minor.*
BORIS VIAN, *Heartsnatcher.*
LLORENÇ VILLALONGA, *The Dolls' Room.*
ORNELA VORPSI, *The Country Where No One Ever Dies.*
AUSTRYN WAINHOUSE, *Hedyphagetica.*
PAUL WEST,
  Words for a Deaf Daughter & Gala.
CURTIS WHITE,
  America's Magic Mountain.
  The Idea of Home.
  Memories of My Father Watching TV.
  Monstrous Possibility: An Invitation to Literary Politics.
  Requiem.
DIANE WILLIAMS, *Excitability: Selected Stories.*
  Romancer Erector.
DOUGLAS WOOLF, *Wall to Wall.*
  Ya! & John-Juan.
JAY WRIGHT, *Polynomials and Pollen.*
  The Presentable Art of Reading Absence.
PHILIP WYLIE, *Generation of Vipers.*
MARGUERITE YOUNG,
  Angel in the Forest.
  Miss MacIntosh, My Darling.
REYOUNG, *Unbabbling.*
VLADO ŽABOT, *The Succubus.*
ZORAN ŽIVKOVIĆ, *Hidden Camera.*
LOUIS ZUKOFSKY, *Collected Fiction.*
SCOTT ZWIREN, *God Head.*

FOR A FULL LIST OF PUBLICATIONS, VISIT:
www.dalkeyarchive.com